GOD'S RADAR

GOD'S RADAR

BY

Fran Arrick

Bradbury Press   Scarsdale, N.Y.

I wish to express my thanks to David L. Edwards and Tom Burbadge for their help and advice. — F.A.

Bradbury Press, Inc.
2 Overhill Road
Scarsdale, N.Y. 10583
An affiliate of Macmillan, Inc.
Collier Macmillan Canada, Inc.
Manufactured in the United States of America
10 9 8 7 6 5 4 3 2 1
The text of this book is set in 11 pt. Galliard.
Library of Congress Cataloging in Publication Data
Arrick, Fran.
God's radar.
Summary: A teen-age girl in a small southern town is torn between her parents' religious rebirth and her boyfriend's free spirit.
I. Title.
PZ7.A74335Go   1983   [Fic]   83-2666
ISBN 0-02-705710-0

GOD'S RADAR

I

At the top of a lone hill, planted like a territorial flag, the radio-and-television transmitting tower glinted in the sunlight. The tall metal structure, all forks and angles, looked out of place rising above the gentle curves of the countryside, but the Cables, whizzing past in their over-loaded station wagon, did not give it even a passing glance.

"Is it all like this?" Roxie asked, leaning forward from the back seat. "All farms and stuff?"

Her father smiled as he drove. "No, Rox, just this small section of the town is rural. In fact, we're right at the edge of a residential section here, see? Lots of houses . . . Then you get into the business section. Nothing's really too far from anything else . . ."

"But you need a car, Frank," his wife said. "We can't just walk to the stores the way we could back home."

"You can," he said, and then conceded, "but it would be a longer walk. See the mountains?" He pointed ahead, toward the windshield. "Aren't they beautiful?"

"Mm-hm," Roxie sighed, leaning against the cardboard carton next to her on the seat. She fought an urge to look back, to see where they had been, where they had come from. She knew it was silly. She couldn't see Syracuse. If she had been able to see through the rear window, past the piles of their belongings, she might have noticed the tower on the hill, silhouetted black now against the sky.

"This is our street, Roxie," Francis Cable called out as he negotiated a sharp right turn. "Here it is, Marian! We're home."

Roxie wriggled uncomfortably on the floor.

Behind her, the projector whirred softly, a steady, soothing sound beneath her mother's bright, staccato narration.

"Oh, look, that's—oh! It's Glenna when she was fourteen! And you were—well, you were seven, right, Roxie? Glenna always took such good care of—oh, see, that's what I mean—the way Glenna caught that ball just as it was about to hit Roxie? Rox? Remember?"

"I remember, Mom . . ." Roxie said, shifting her position again. "But maybe the Pregers—" she wrinkled her nose—"are a little bored with strangers' home movies . . ."

"Oh, no, Roxie!" Cynthia Preger assured her. She was sitting on the couch between Roxie's mother and her own daughter, Bess. "I think this is a lovely way to get to know new neighbors, don't you, Bess?"

"Yes, it's fun," Bess agreed.

Mmmm, sure, Roxie thought. She could picture her friends Ellie and Marge, back in Syracuse, being shown home movies by a new girl on the block! Probably they'd giggle all the way home. And Bess Preger was fifteen, the same age . . .

"Look!" Roxie's mother cried. "That's Glenna, making that awful face at the camera!"

Roxie had to smile at her older sister's face, with it's silly crossed eyes and protruding tongue, grinning down at her from the bed sheet Marian had tacked up to serve as a screen.

"Glenna's not with y'all now?" Cynthia Preger asked.

"No, Glenna's all of twenty-two now and on her own." Marian shook her head and smiled. "It's hard to believe how fast they grow up. Glenna moved to New York City when we moved down here . . ." She glanced at the flickering screen. "I do hope this isn't boring you . . . We unpacked all these things just this afternoon and I wanted to see the movies anyway, since we'd just be storing them away again—"

"Not at all," Cynthia repeated. "It's nice of y'all to share them with us."

"I think the coffee's ready," Roxie said. "I can smell it, Mom . . ."

Her father emerged from the basement with Bess's father at that moment, much to Roxie's relief.

"You still showing those movies?" Francis Cable asked with a grin. "I'm surprised you girls aren't asleep by now!"

"We enjoyed it," Cynthia said.

"It was just one movie, Frank . . ."

"Only because you don't know how to change reels, Marian," her husband said.

"I'm awful about things like that, too," Cynthia Preger said with a smile.

Marian stood up. "Well, I guess the coffee's ready." She parted the drapes, and the late afternoon sun streamed into the living room. "I'm dying to try your lovely cake, Cynthia. It was so nice of you to bring it. Roxie, would you and Bess like some cake or would you rather go up to your room and get to know each other?"

Roxie knew what Marge and Ellie and her other friends would rather do!

"I guess we'll go upstairs, okay?" She smiled conspiratorially at Bess.

"All right," Bess said.

"I was telling Frank I wasn't sure about a couple of spots in the basement, Marian. Best to have an exterminator in, just to be sure," Joe Preger was saying as Roxie and Bess climbed the stairs.

"It's a real nice room," Bess said softly. She was still standing in the doorway while Roxie plopped onto her bed with a sigh of relief.

"Thanks. Listen, I'm really sorry about that stuff downstairs. Home movies! Not *too* embarrassing! Especially when they're a hundred years old!"

"I didn't mind," Bess said. "Really."

Roxie lifted a carton of clothes off the bed and patted the place where it had been.

"Sit," she offered. "It's not 'home' yet, but I'm working on it."

Bess sat gingerly. "I was in this room only once before," she said. "The people who lived here didn't have any kids, but one time I helped the lady carry a chair up here. "Where did y'all move from?" Bess asked.

"Syracuse. New York."

"Ohhh . . . New York?"

"It's not like New York City," Roxie said quickly, not knowing what Bess thought of New York City. "In fact it's not—well, it's not *too* much bigger than Howerton."

"Oh, really?"

"Uh-huh."

There was silence then, and Roxie felt responsible. She began to chatter.

"But it was home to me since I was four and I felt awful about having to leave, you know, when the plant transferred my father . . . But my sister, Glenna, she said that change was good, that we all need change every now and then to help us grow . . ." Her voice trailed off.

"Why didn't your sister move with you?" Bess asked.

"I wish she had," Roxie said. "But she's been finished with school about a year now and she wanted to go to New York City and find a job. I really miss her . . ."

"I have an older sister, too," Bess said. "But she lives at home. Well, at the college, really, but she comes home a lot. When she graduates, she wants to go into service."

"Into the army?" Roxie asked, her eyes widening.

"No," Bess answered and smiled. "Into service. For the Lord."

"Oh," Roxie answered, her eyes wider still.

"She has a really beautiful voice and she sings in the church choir. They've traveled all over the world, practically."

"Your church choir?"

"Yes, you've probably seen them on television. They're on television a lot, all over the country. Sunday mornings? Saturdays?"

"Uh, well, maybe . . ."

"You should hear them," Bess said. "Oh, they're so good!"

Roxie stayed in her room after Bess and her parents left. She wanted some time to herself. This was just their third day in the new house and already two sets of neighbors had come to call and welcome them. Maybe, she thought, that's how people are in the South; it was never like that in Syracuse. The new kids made friends, but not because their neighbors dropped in with cakes and homemade fudge and plants. New kids made friends at school—the way Roxie planned to do when it began. Still, it was only the beginning of the summer and it was nice that Bess lived next door . . .

Roxie opened the carton she'd put on the floor near her bed. It was the one in which she'd packed all her special, private things. Smiling to herself, she lifted out the thick newspaper wrappings that protected her favorite framed photographs.

The first was a five-by-seven, color picture of herself and Peter Quinn in their prom clothes—her ninth-grade graduation-from-junior-high prom.

Peter had looked so terrific in his white dinner jacket . . . And Roxie, still smiling, thought she looked terrific, too, in her yellow . . . She'd sat in the sun with Glenna's reflector through all of May and most of June, her heart set on a beautiful tan to contrast with that off-the-shoulder canary-colored chiffon . . .

Carefully, she stood the picture on her night table and took out the next one: a group picture of all her friends, taken at the going-away party Marge had thrown in her basement for Roxie.

Roxie looked at the expression on Peter Quinn's face in the picture. He was saying, "You'll make new friends so fast, Rox, you'll forget all about us . . ."

"I won't, Peter, I won't ever forget you . . ." With a little sigh, Roxie put that picture next to the other and took out the last: a photo of her family, taken in their backyard just before Glenna left for New York City. "Don't be sad, Rox—we'll be together every holiday and I'll write and you'll write . . ."

"I'll miss you, Glen . . ."

"Me, too, baby sister . . ."

Well, she thought, it *is* a friendly town. That couple who visited yesterday was nice, the Pregers were nice . . .

Roxie hugged herself and glanced around her new room. It was a good size. Big enough to invite her girlfriends up so they could all sit on the carpeted floor and talk and eat . . .

Her mind kept coming back to Bess Preger. She thought Bess was rather pretty, with her longish blonde hair flipped back along the sides and her wide blue eyes . . . She reminded Roxie a little of her friend Ellie from home. No. Not "home" any more . . . Not any more . . . Roxie shook her head, as if to clear it.

From the way Bess spoke about her sister, Roxie

gathered she was probably fairly religious. The Cables had belonged to the Presbyterian Church in Syracuse, and though the family hadn't attended every Sunday, still, they were members in good standing and helped with fund-raising drives and the aid society, and Roxie's mother had attended a Bible study group for a while . . .

Roxie made a clicking noise with her tongue. She'd forgotten to ask Bess what kids their age did when they weren't in school—where they went, where they hung out. If one had to drive to get anywhere in Howerton, she wondered how everyone under the driving age managed.

But Bess hadn't seemed as if she were bored living in Howerton. Bess had said Roxie would love living there.

Roxie hoped so. She wanted to love living in Howerton. She wanted to like Bess Preger.

"They belong to the Stafford Hill Baptist Church," Marian explained to Roxie at dinner. "They're very active in it. They said everyone is enormously friendly. Cynthia wanted to know which church we'd joined."

"You tell her we'd like to unpack first?" Francis Cable said, smiling as he sipped his coffee.

"I guess I said something like that," his wife said with a laugh. "But I do think it's lovely how friendly the people are. The—uh—what was their name, Frank, the people who stopped over yesterday? With the plant?"

"Hefferberg? Hepplewhite?"

"Heffernan. They belong to Stafford Hill, too. Did

you know that their Sunday service is televised every week?"

"Oh, *that's* why Bess said her sister—"

"What, Rox?"

"Bess Preger said her sister sings in a church choir on television," Roxie explained.

Her father nodded. "Sure, that's Caraman's church. He's always in the news. You've heard of him, Marian, I'm sure . . ."

Marian scratched her head. "Caraman . . . Oh, yes! I *have* heard of him. I don't think I've ever seen him, though. Have you, Roxie?"

"Uh-uh."

Francis dabbed at the side of his mouth with his napkin. "Mmm, he's a big evangelist . . . Speaks out a lot. Politically, I mean. He takes tough stands, supports candidates, makes speeches. I've seen him once or twice on TV. Very charismatic guy, as they say."

"Clement Caraman?" Roxie asked suddenly.

"Yes, that's right."

"Oh, I know about him," Roxie said. "We talked about him in current events last winter. When the prayer-in-schools thing came up. We had a debate about it and one of the kids quoted him."

"Was he for or against?" Francis asked.

"Oh, Francis!" Marian laughed. "You're kidding!"

"Of course I'm kidding," he said. "Putting prayer back in the public schools was one of his biggest campaigns. Who won your debate, Rox?"

"Nobody won," Roxie said with a shrug. "Jack Tyler and Rob McVey got into a fist fight over it and so we decided to discuss something else."

"A fist fight. Really?" her father said. "That's interesting . . . A brawl over a subject like prayer."

"Mmmm," Roxie agreed. "I guess I never thought of it that way."

II

Francis was able to settle into his work routine almost immediately so most of the unpacking was left to Roxie and her mother. But once things were in place, there was little for them to do. A week after they'd moved in, they decided to explore their new town and saw everything there was to see in two afternoons and a morning.

Marian bought Roxie a blouse at Milly's Boutique on Main Street in the "city" part of Howerton. She felt obligated to buy something when Roxie unthinkingly wailed, "Is this the *only* clothing store in the whole town?"

Caroline Freely, the owner, bristled. "Well, honey, I may not have all the Paris fashions, but I carry all what they're wearin' in Wash'nin' and I do have some love-ly things that came from N'Yawk . . ."

"The clothes *are* lovely," Marian said, nudging Roxie's sandled foot with her toe. "My daughter's just used to a large city with about twenty stores of one kind on a single block!" She laughed, but Caroline didn't join her. "Well . . ." Marian said lamely, "we've just moved

. . . Oh, Roxie, this blouse is just your style! Try it on!"

"You would've bought it if it had one long sleeve and one short and was covered with plastic daisies!" Roxie told her mother when they were back on the street.

Marian smiled. "You bet I would've," she said. "Roxie, you can't come down here like some big northern snob and start criticizing. That's no way to win friends and influence people . . ."

"Oh, I wasn't criticizing," Roxie grumbled. "I was just in shock. You look up the street and down the street and there's the whole city!"

"Shall we try the next block?" Marian asked hopefully.

"There *is* no next block!"

The day before, they'd visited Roxie's new high school on Marble Avenue. The principal's secretary showed them some classrooms, the gym and the auditorium and then left them to explore on their own.

"Nice," Marian said and her voice echoed in the empty hall.

"It's eerie," Roxie said. "Isn't a school eerie when it's empty?"

"It's very modern," her mother said, nodding toward a glassed-in corridor with plants hanging from a long rod near the ceiling.

"Mmmm," Roxie said.

"It's a newer building than Dyer . . . Rox?"

"What?"

"I said, it's a newer building than Dyer High. Back home. This is *newer*. Honestly, Roxie, aren't you paying atten—"

"I am. I am. Yes, it's nice." She giggled. "It's just so

spooky! I bet if Ellie were here, or Marge, we'd be running around writing things on all the blackboards . . ." She laughed out loud. "I won't tell you what things!"

"Roxie, really!" Marian made a face.

During the two and a half days of what Roxie and her mother called "the Howerton Expedition," they'd eaten lunch at the Pizza Hut, Arby's and Howard Johnson's, which were all on the interstate highway.

At the Pizza Hut, a young waiter loaded Roxie's pizza with extra meatballs and winked at her to let her know.

"Welcome to Howerton," he said.

"How'd you know we just got here?" Roxie asked, tilting her head.

"One, your ac-cent, and two, I know all the other pretty girls in this town."

Roxie rolled her eyes.

"I'm Orrin Briley, who're you?"

"Roxie Cable."

"Hi," he said. She heard "Hah!"

"Hah!" she said.

"Now, you makin' fun?" Orrin asked.

"No, I'm just trying to fit in," she said, and smiled.

"Are you in high school?" Marian asked Orrin.

"No, ma'am, I just graduated in June. But I have a sister there. She's goin' into tenth grade . . . Name's Mary Carol Briley."

"Marble Avenue?" Roxie asked.

"Yep."

"I'll probably meet her then. I'm going into tenth, too."

"I woulda thought you were a college girl," Orrin said.

Roxie, who wasn't sure if he was kidding, decided

she's resist the impulse to pick up a meatball with her fingers.

Francis Cable, an engineer with Arroway-Electric, rarely had occasion to visit that part of Howerton people referred to as "the city." He was absorbed in his work and the newness of his surroundings, the differences between the Howerton plant and the one in Syracuse, the layouts of the laboratories, his new associates. The novelty was stimulating, challenging. He felt a sense of forward motion.

The "city" moved, but at a quieter pace. On Main Street, everyone knew what he was about, whom he would see and just what kind of business his store or restaurant could be expected to do on a given day. And there was always time for a break—a rest, a chat, a cup of coffee.

Lew Hawley drove downtown each morning at seven-forty-five with Thomas John Seeds in a dilapidated Ford pickup. Seeds opened his newsstand at eight, and though Lew's Thom Mc An shoe store didn't officially open until nine, he enjoyed the ride, having coffee in the Quik-Stop and reading his paper before starting his workday. His routine was the same, his conversations, the same.

"Hey, Tommy-John, how are y'all this morning?"

"All right, Lew . . . All right . . ."

"Hot one today."

"Looks to be."

"How's Eileen?"

"All right . . . Wanda?"

"She's fine, just fine. Your boy and girls?"

"Boy's working. Construction over at the camp. The little one's there, too. Molly, well, she's not doing much, got to keep the eye on her . . . How's your girl?"

"Oh, she's all right. Comes in to work for me afternoons. Good girl, Louise is." He waved from the truck's window. "There's Caroline, opening up Milly's. Why don't she change the name of that store, anyway? Milly sold out to her two years ago!"

"Three."

"Three, huh?"

Seeds parked in an alley lot and they both grunted as they got out of the truck.

"Coffee today, Tommy-John?"

"Nope. Gotta open."

"Well, open then, and let's have a paper."

Together they opened Seeds' newsstand. Lew picked up a copy of the *Howerton Sun & Chronicle,* flipped a coin at Seeds, who was turning on his air conditioner, and muttered at the headline.

"World's sure goin' to Hell in a basket, Tommy-John . . ."

"Sure is, Lew. Sure is."

"Well . . . I'll see you at prayer meeting."

"You can count on that, Lew!"

At the Quik-Stop, Lew teased the waitress who always brought him his coffee-light-toasted-English.

"Hey, Doris, pretty girl like you still wastin' your time pourin' coffee?"

"Now what else 'm I gonna do, Lew Hawley?"

"You write your letter yet, Doris?"

"Which letter's that?"

"The one to your state senator, the one Dr. Caraman told us to write last week, the one about the taxpayers' money goin' to libraries that carry all those dirty books."

"Oh, *that* letter."

"That's the one, Doris. Y'all better write it, you know—you got a little tyke of your own be goin' to that public library 'fore you know it. Now it's important, Doris."

"I know it is, Lew. I will write it."

"You do that, Doris. Praise Jesus."

"Praise Jesus, Lew."

Lew looked around the Quik-Stop to see who had come in before they went to work or to shop. He smiled and waved at those he knew and asked about their families, commented on the weather and settled finally in a booth to read his paper.

"The Howerton Exedition" joke between Roxie and her mother wore thin as Roxie found herself spending much of her time alone on her front porch. She read books, played solitaire, sniffed the heavy southern-summer air, while Marian fussed with flower borders at the sides of the house and a rock garden in the back.

One weekday morning in mid-July, Marian called to Roxie from the kitchen. Sighing, Roxie struggled to her feet from the porch floor, rubbing her bare thigh where it had stuck to the painted wood. She pulled open the screen door and yelled, "What?" in a bored voice.

"Why don't you go next door and see what Bess is doing today?" Marian called.

Roxie sighed again. "She's in camp," she called back.

"I don't think so—not Wednesdays. She's only there part time . . . Why don't you try?"

"Well . . . Okay . . ."

Without bothering to put on shoes or change out of shorts, Roxie closed the door again and tramped across the grass to the Pregers'.

"Hello, Roxie!" Cynthia Preger greeted her. "It's nice to see you! Did you want Bess?"

Roxie attempted a smile and nodded.

"Well, she'll be right back, honey. She's over at the church Xeroxing something for the bus ministry. Would you like to come in and wait?"

"Well, uh—"

Bess's mother opened the door wider and stepped back. "Now you just come on in. I'm baking fresh oatmeal-raisin cookies and a cinnamon coffee cake, and if you help, you get to taste."

Roxie smelled the cinnamon and it made her mouth water, but she wondered why Mrs. Preger would pick such a hot day to bake.

"I know it's awful hot to have the oven going like this," Cynthia said as if reading Roxie's mind, "but I've got the air conditioning on in the living room and the kitchen has a big fan in it. We're having some neighbors over tonight after prayer meeting."

"Oh . . ."

"I'm really hoping we get central air conditioning one day soon," Cynthia went on. "Joe's been promising for years now, but it seems there's always something more important to spend our money on . . . isn't that always the way? Well, I guess your mama and daddy know, with two growing girls in the family, just like ours . . .

Roxie, honey, would y'all like to spoon these out on that cookie sheet for me while I do this one?" Cynthia handed Roxie a bowl. "Make them just about the size of a half dollar?" Roxie noticed that most of Cynthia's sentences ended with a rising inflection.

"What's a bus ministry, Mrs. Preger?" she asked, as she spooned dough onto the cookie sheet.

"Well, honey, many people aren't able or aren't willing to come to church so we just go to them, you know, trying to win souls for Jesus, trying to make people see that the Bible is the only true road to salvation. Our church, Stafford Hill? Well, we have hundreds of volunteers in just about every area you can imagine. Why, we do wonderful work with children, with the handicapped, with senior citizens . . . We're just sending people all over!"

Roxie nodded and spooned.

"I know you folks were churchgoers back in Syracuse. Your mama told me," Cynthia said.

"Uh-huh . . ."

"I know you're not Fundamentalists, though . . ."

"Presbyterian," Roxie said.

"Well, yes, honey, but what I mean is—well, it doesn't even matter what religion you are, if you accept Jesus Christ and the Bible and all it has to say." Cynthia put down her bowl and leaned back against the sink. "You know, Roxie . . . I've been wanting to ask your parents to come with us to one of our prayer meetings. And you, too, of course. I wanted to ask you all right away, after we visited, but then Joe had to be out of town for ten days and I wanted us all to go together the first time. It's so nice when you go as a family, that's what

it's all about, really, the family? Keepin' the family together?" She smiled. Roxie smiled back.

"Anyway," Cynthia continued, "tonight it would be
just wonderful if y'all could come because the get-to-
gether's at our house afterward and you could meet so
many nice people. Do you think y'all'd like that?"

Roxie shrugged. She wanted to be polite and not hurt
her new neighbor's feelings. But she knew that if someone back in Syracuse had suggested a prayer meeting as
an activity, she and her friends would have giggled. She
wanted to giggle now, but she didn't. Instead, she
spooned some dough onto the cookie sheet and asked
noncommittally, "What's it like? Prayer meeting . . ."

"Prayer meeting? Oh, it's lovely, it really is. Dr. Caraman is just so stirring, so fascinating to listen to, and
they always have a few youngsters from Christian Grace
College to sing, like our Patty, and sometimes there's a
guest speaker and there are announcements, you know,
about what's going on in the community and where we
can all be of help—well, just *lots* of things! It's so inspir-
ing, Roxie. You should just hear Dr. Caraman! Make
that one a little larger, dear." She pointed to Roxie's last
spooned cookie.

Roxie brushed some hair from her forehead with the
back of her wrist and wondered what to say. Maybe, she
thought, this is just the way they do things down
here . . .

She decided to shift the whole question onto Marian's
shoulders.

"Well, I guess you could ask my mother," she said,
not looking at Cynthia. "She's—" She stopped as the
front door slammed and Bess called that she was home.

"In the kitchen, dear!" Cynthia said. "And Roxie's here!"

Bess bounced in with a flushed face, her flipped hair damp.

"Hi!" she said to Roxie.

"Hi, Bess . . ."

"Here's the pile," Bess said, putting a large stack of papers on the kitchen table. "I made twelve hundred, like you said."

"Mmmmm . . ." Cynthia mused. "I wonder if I should have told you more."

"Uh!" Bess grunted. "Do I have to go back?"

Her mother sighed. "No . . . I guess it should be enough. Nadine told me twelve hundred and she should know . . . She's done it enough times herself."

"What are they?" Roxie asked.

"These? They're prayer sheets," Bess said. "It's a list of people who need to be prayed for. Here." She handed one to Roxie, who read lists of names in various categories: sick, out of work, drug-involved, starting churches—

" 'Ministries,' " Roxie read aloud.

"Mm-hm, like the bus ministry I told you about," Cynthia said. "And there's a youth ministry, a telephone ministry—that's for witnessing to people over the phone—there's a counseling ministry, a home for alcoholics, one for unwed mothers—"

"We pray for all the ministries, too," Bess said. "Everything on the sheet."

"I've asked Roxie and her family to come with us tonight," Cynthia said, smiling. "I haven't spoken to her mama yet, but I'm going to right now."

"Oh!" Bess said brightly. "That's good, Roxie!"

"Well . . . I don't know yet," Roxie hedged. "I guess it's up to my parents . . ."

"The first batch of cookies will be ready in a few minutes," Cynthia said. "I think there's enough for you girls to enjoy a few. Why don't you go out back to the hammock and I'll bring them out in a while with some lemonade?"

"Fine," Bess said.

Roxie said, "Okay . . ."

"Do you know Orrin Briley?" Roxie asked. She rocked the huge mesh hammock with her grounded leg; the other one was curled underneath her as she leaned back.

"Briley? I don't think so . . . Who is he?"

"He's a waiter at the Pizza Hut," Roxie said. "I thought he was cute. Graduated high school in June."

"Marble Avenue or Brighton?" Bess asked.

"Marble . . ."

"Oh. I know some kids from there. But I go to S.H.C.A."

Roxie sat up. "You don't go to Marble?" she asked.

"No, I thought I told you. Stafford Hill Christian Academy. It's with the church. It's a private school."

"Oh!" Roxie sat back. She'd assumed Bess went to the same school she'd be attending. "Maybe you did tell me and I just didn't catch it . . . I guess I was thinking of your sister . . ."

"She went to Stafford Hill, too, but now she's at Christian Grace . . ."

"Oh," Roxie said again.

"I don't go to the Pizza Hut much," Bess said.

Roxie rocked the hammock a little harder. "What's your job like?" she asked after a while. "The one at the camp?"

"Oh, it's not a job, really. I'm sort of a volunteer," Bess answered. "I help out in the crafts shop, mostly, but I work in the office and the animal shelter and sometimes I do a Bible class . . ."

"It's a religious camp?" Roxie asked. She suddenly missed her friends Marge and Ellie very much.

"Well, yes, it's part of Stafford Hill. Dr. Caraman built it. It's only about twelve years old, but it gets bigger and better every year. They even have tennis courts now, and way down at one end, they're building a big gym! It's really nice for the kids."

Roxie closed her eyes. She inhaled the scent of flowers but she didn't know what they were. She decided they smelled large. And purple.

She opened her eyes when she realized she was in danger of falling asleep in a stranger's backyard, with the stranger next to her.

"What do you do around here?" she asked Bess. "I mean, when you're not going to church or something?"

"Well, I help out at home . . . We have a lot of homework during school, I have a Bible studies group, we go on church picnics and backpacking groups, I babysit . . . I work on some of the ministries . . ."

"How about other kids?" Roxie asked. "Do you have friends? A group? You know . . ."

Now it was Bess's turn to put her foot down and swing the hammock.

"Oh, yes," she said. "But we don't do a lot of the stuff that public school kids do because we separate from the world. We don't need to conform to fads and things, like rock 'n' roll or drinking or drugs . . . We're a society apart."

"My friends didn't do drugs," Roxie said quickly. "But we—"

"What?" Bess asked.

"Well, we liked to dance . . ." She decided to change the subject. "Is there a movie theater around?" she asked. "I think I've been all over Howerton and I didn't see one."

"There's one in Annenville," Bess said. "That's the closest. But we don't go."

"You don't go to the movies?"

"No. See, Roxie, when you've taken the Lord into your heart, you don't need that worldly stuff filling up your mind. We're not interested in the immorality that Hollywood wants us to watch. And we do a lot of things as a family . . ." She sat up and looked at Roxie, who had closed her eyes again. "The family is the backbone of the country . . ." she said.

Roxie was never so glad to see oatmeal cookies and lemonade, when Bess's mother brought out the tray. She finally had fallen asleep for a few minutes and was thankful that Bess had not realized it.

"What do you think, Frank, do you want to go?" Marian asked, after he'd heard about Cynthia's invitation.

"Oh, boy," he said.

"You should have heard what Roxie said," his wife told him.

"I can imagine." He put his briefcase on the hall table and tapped it. "I did bring home some work here that I should do tonight . . ." he said.

"I was going to write letters."

"I don't know, Marian, I feel funny about it . . . Prayer meeting?"

"I guess I do, too. I hate to turn down their invitation, though, after they've been so nice . . . And we do want to join a church—maybe we should see what this one is like . . ."

He sat heavily in a chair. "I guess one evening won't kill us." He scratched his head and thought for a moment. "You know, I think I *would* like to hear Caraman in person. Should be interesting. Roxie upstairs?"

Marian nodded.

"*Rox?*" he called. "Come on down!"

He was smiling as his daughter leaned over the banister.

"Hi, Daddy . . ."

"Hi, babe. You want to do this thing tonight with us?" he asked. "Your mother and I think it would be nice for the Pregers and I really wouldn't mind listening to this guy Caraman. He's getting to be a pretty well known evangelist or whatever they call them . . . What do you say?"

Roxie didn't say.

"Aw, come on, Rox," her father encouraged. "I'm kind of curious now, aren't you? Something to write to your friends about?"

"Let's just see what it's like," her mother urged. "You'll

be with Bess, you'll probably meet some other kids, too . . ."

"You know she doesn't go to my school?" Roxie said. "She goes to the church academy."

"Well, honey, are you only supposed to be friends with your schoolmates?" Marian asked. "Come on. She's a nice enough girl. And our neighbors . . ."

Roxie wrinkled her nose.

"Glory be, Roseanne, can't you hear the call?" Francis leaped up on the sofa and spread his arms. "Can't you *hear* it? *Please,* let this girl see the light . . ." He clapped his palms together and turned his face toward the ceiling.

"Francis, now you stop that," Marian said with a smile and Roxie was giggling.

"Okay, Daddy, okay," she said. "I'll go, I'll go . . ."

"A-men and hal-le-LU-jah!" Francis cried, jumping off the couch.

Roxie changed from her shorts to a red denim skirt and the blouse that Marian had bought at Milly's Boutique—white cotton with a small pink bow at the collar. Marian wore a seersucker suit and Francis retied his tie.

"This feels like Sunday," Roxie complained. "How many people do you think will be there on a Wednesday night?"

III

The Stafford Hill Baptist Church was at the top of a steep incline on a one-way street. Everyone driving away from the church was forced to continue on Stafford Hill Road, heading straight down the incline, a point of topography which had caused a church member to remark that once you were out from under the roof of Stafford Hill, you just kept sinking toward Hell.

The Cables, sitting in the Pregers' station wagon, all gasped at their first view.

"What was that you asked about the number of people that would show up?" Francis asked Roxie, his jaw dropping in surprise.

"We missed this on 'the Howerton Expedition,'" Roxie whispered to him.

The church had two parking lots, one adjoining its buildings complex, the other across the street. Both lots were of shopping-center size and both were filled. Teenage boys were stationed at the entrances as well as throughout the lots to direct cars.

Behind the wheel, Joe Preger grinned.

"We usually get between three and four thousand people at prayer meeting," he said. "On Sundays more . . ."

"I had no idea," Marian breathed, gaping out the window.

"See? That's the school, the S.H.C.A.—that big white brick building in back," Bess said, pointing to a structure connected to the church by a steel canopy and cement walk. "And there's the main sanctuary down there. That's the gym, where they have the junior church."

"Did you folks bring your own Bibles?" Joe asked as he squeezed his car into a small space.

"Don't they have them on the pews in front of you?" Francis asked.

"No, here we bring our own."

"I'm sorry. I should have mentioned it," Cynthia said. "We mark special passages in our own Bibles, the ones Dr. Caraman talks about, so we can remember just what he said. You'll see why when you hear him."

"We—are—so—glad—to—see—you!" Clement Caraman shouted from the pulpit. "We are so glad you're here among us, so glad we're together on this lovely southern summer night under God's heaven and in God's own church. And this *is* God's own church!"

Someone yelled, "Amen!" Roxie turned around and decided it had been a large man with a red face, two pews behind.

"*This* is the church where you will hear the gospel preached, the gospel adhered to, the pure saving gospel of Jesus Christ! The word! The *Truth!*

"Your apostate churches do not preach the pure saving gospel of Jesus Christ because it is unpopular! The truth, my friends, is unpopular! To preach against the murder of thousands of unborn babies is unpopular! To preach against the splitting of families is unpopular! To preach against homosexuals teaching our children is unpopular! To teach the science of creationism is unpopular!"

The red-faced man yelled, "Amen!" again and Francis smiled.

Then Dr. Caraman dropped his voice to a hoarse whisper.

"In this church I preach the truth, though it may be un-pop-ular. That is what you will hear at Stafford Hill, my friends. America doesn't need apostate churches, doesn't need pol-i-ticians—" his voice rose—"doesn't *need* all those institutions of higher learning causing our young people to question the true way! America doesn't *need* the widespread use of drugs! America doesn't *need* the spread of secular humanism! America needs to wake up to what's going on! Let us wake up, America!" Now he was shouting: "Cancel that bridge game, cancel that tennis party, cancel that bowling league tournament, turn off those immoral television programs! America, get down on your knees, get *down* on your knees and let *Jesus* come into your hearts! Wake *up*, America!"

"I'm up," Francis whispered to Marian.

Dr. Caraman again lowered his voice. "Let us begin this evening by singing hymn 341."

"He's only *beginning*," Roxie whispered to her father, who squeezed her hand.

She didn't know the hymn. She tried to mouth the

words as she looked around her surreptitiously. There were no very young children, but there were many teen-agers and their parents. Many older people, too. Each person was singing, each voice loud and full. They were accompanied by an orchestra that seemed to surround them and make the sound of the hymn sweeter, clearer.

"Terrific sound system," Francis, who would notice such things, whispered to his wife. "Must've cost a for-tune!"

"We have many new friends with us tonight," Cara-man said, holding aloft a handful of orange guest cards, one of which had been filled in by the Cables. "I want to take a moment now to welcome our visitors and re-new our love for the Lord and each other. Each and every one of you—turn around and shake the hand of the person behind you, the person in front of you, the person on each side of you! Jesus loves each one of you and you love whom Jesus loves!"

Roxie smiled as her father shook her hand.

"Jesus is there, in every phase of your life, and He wants you to rejoice no matter what because He is greater than the circumstances of your life! Jesus is your answer, your only answer, your only answer is *Jesus,* my friends!"

Francis looked at his watch.

"Tonight," Dr. Caraman continued, "I'm going to talk to you about my soul-winning mission to South Amer-ica, from which I've just returned and about which I'm sure you've read in your newspapers. I'm going to tell you what it felt like to walk hand in hand with little children and watch them feel the presence of Christ in their hearts for the very first time. But before I do that,

I want you to enjoy the lovely voices of our own little Joannie Campbell and that funny-looking geezer she met while attending C.G.C., Tom Birkenhead!" Everybody laughed, especially the family of the funny-looking geezer. Roxie decided he was the handsomest boy she'd ever seen. She also thought Joannie Campbell looked a lot like Bess, with her blonde hair flipped along the sides. And then she noticed that most of the young girls and young women also had blonde hair, flipped back at the sides.

"Joannie and Tom, here, were with me on my trip, along with the other singers from the Christian Grace Choir, and their young voices and the words that they were singing were just about the finest inspiration those folks could have had. The people just loved them—and now they're back with us and ready to be an inspiration to you, too! Joannie? Tom?"

"What did you think, Frank?" Marian whispered. They were standing in a corner of the Pregers' air-conditioned living room while a small crowd of people buzzed and hummed around them.

". . . That this punch isn't even spiked. I guess they don't drink at all," her husband answered.

"No, really," she said. "I meant about the meeting."

"I know," he smiled. "Well, I wasn't bored. Were you?"

Cynthia Preger suddenly materialized next to them with a tray of cookies.

"Say, you two, what are you whispering about? Have one of these luscious things. Your daughter baked them!"

Obligingly, the Cables each took a cookie.

"Now, I'll be back in just a minute," Cynthia said, "as soon as I take these around. There are some folks I want y'all to meet." She bustled off.

"No," Marian said in answer to her husband's question, "I wasn't bored. Far from it."

"You think those political stands he takes belong in church?" Francis asked.

Marian shrugged. "I don't know . . . He puts it all in the context of moral issues and quotes the Bible—"

"And *quotes* the Bible! Boy, to hear him, you'd think there's something in there for every problem in the world! Why don't you look up how to kill those bugs on your marigolds?"

"Oh, Francis . . ."

"Ah! Or what about those bugs in the new Arroway toaster-oven?"

"Frank, be serious—"

"You two can't just stand here giggling by yourselves," Cynthia interrupted, once again at their side. "Now I want you to come over here and hear what this group has to say. It's a committee we've organized to collect things for the new church retirement home." She took Marian's arm and began to steer them toward the center of the room. "Oh, Roxie!" she called, as the girl passed them. "Are you going outside? Take some cake out for the others, won't you, dear?"

Roxie sat with four girls, including Bess, all entering tenth grade at Stafford Hill Christian Academy. They were out at the Pregers' hammock again, sitting in a row, with plates of cinnamon coffee cake and plastic cups of lemonade or punch on the grass at their feet.

"Did you like Dr. Caraman, Roxie?" one of the girls asked. Her name was Hope and Roxie liked her friendly smile.

"Do you?" Roxie asked, diplomatically reserving her opinion.

Hope nodded as she sipped her lemonade. ". . . Except he can be really strict. Especially if he walks into your class and sees all the kids talking or something."

"Ooooh, yes!" a girl called Lee-Ann agreed. "One time during Old Testament survey? He came in and dragged Steve Kreske out by the collar for sending a paper airplane across the room!" She giggled. "It hit Dr. Caraman right in the chest!"

"Oh, Steve Kreske!" Bess said with a small wave of her fingers. "He's been suspended a thousand times."

"What for?" Roxie asked.

"Oh, smoking, swearing, cutting classes," Hope answered. "But they're always looking to catch Steve. Lots of kids break the rules but nothing much happens to them . . ."

"They get punished," Bess said.

"Not Kenny and Jarrell. They never got suspended or anything. Detention sometimes, but that's all."

"Who are Kenny and Jarrell?" Roxie asked.

Lee-Ann made a face and shrugged. "Just some boys who like to shock people. But they're kind of funny, though, so they don't get reported on usually."

Roxie said, "Reported on?"

"Well, we're on sort of an honor system. It's for everyone's own good, really. If you see someone doing something that's against God's pleasure you're supposed to report him. Some people report a lot and some don't . . ."

A quiet girl whose name was Louise said, "Jarrell's been reported on a few times. Kenny, too . . ."

"And Molly Seeds and Jennifer Goulding . . ." Lee-Ann said.

"Well, *Molly*," Louise sniffed. "Everyone knows about her."

"Lots of kids do crazy things when they get away from their parents or the school," Lee-Ann said.

"But with Jarrell or Kenny," Louise said, "it's a little different because kids like them. They make you laugh, especially Jarrell."

"You mean *you* like him, Louise," Hope teased.

Louise ignored her, digging into her cake with her fork. "If their parents ever found out, they'd get killed," she said.

"Especially Jarrell's," Bess added. "Can you imagine Mr. Meek finding out that Jarrell drinks about a six-pack every single night?"

"Who told you that, Bess?" Louise said.

"Oh, everyone knows that, Louise." Bess turned to Roxie. "But Jarrell's so pious when he talks to Dr. Caraman or Mrs. Bates or Dr. Arman or any of the teachers, you'd think he did nothing but spend his time in devotions to the Lord!"

The girls all laughed except Louise, who turned to Roxie and asked, "Is Roxie your real name? It's so different."

"Roseanne," Roxie answered, "but my sister called me Roxie from the time I was a baby."

"They'll probably call you Roseanne in school. Because it sounds more dignified," Hope said. "But the kids'll call you Roxie if you want . . ."

"She's not going to Stafford. She's going to Marble," Bess said quickly.

The other three girls looked at Roxie.

"Marble?" Lee-Ann asked. "I thought you were going to S.H.C.A."

Roxie shrugged and made an apologetic face.

"Well," Bess said, putting her empty glass on her paper plate, "God has a purpose for everything. And there's a purpose in your being here with us, Roxie—in Howerton, in your house, at prayer meeting, at *our* house tonight. And we'll find out what that purpose is as God unfolds his plan step by step, right?" She smiled at her friends.

"Amen," Louise whispered and smiled back.

IV

A special minibus, leaving from the parking lot at the Stafford Hill Church, took Bess Preger and the other part-time day workers out to Camp Deliverance in the mornings and brought them back each afternoon at five. The counselors and campers lived at the camp, which was situated on a small lake—also called Deliverance—six miles west of Howerton.

On the Friday morning after the prayer meeting, Bess, with permission from the camp director, brought Roxie with her to help out and look around.

Roxie was glad to go.

She was doing nothing at home and the other three girls she had met at Bess's were all working. Hope was a counselor at Camp Deliverance, Lee-Ann was a mother's helper and Louise worked in her father's shoe store each afternoon.

Roxie had worn through her deck of cards, written countless letters to Peter, Ellie and Marge in Syracuse and read enough books to make her eyes cross.

Bess's invitation represented a change and Roxie wasn't much concerned about what kind of change it was.

The bus bounced over a rough dirt road past a security guard who waved it through, and it squealed and grunted to a stop in a cul-de-sac at the foot of the main building.

"That's the office and it's attached to the dining hall," Bess explained as they got out of the bus. "Down that way are the cabins and the activity buildings. We'll go to the office first and I'll introduce you and get my assignments, okay?"

Roxie's hand was clenched in a firm, warm grip by the camp director, Herbert deGroot, who encouraged her to wander anywhere she liked to and to meet everyone.

"Why don't you start out with me at the crafts cabin," Bess suggested, "and then see if there's something else you'd like to do."

"Fine," Roxie agreed. "I like crafts."

They began a leisurely walk toward the building, where Bess's assignment was to help two groups of ten-year-olds make ceramic plaques.

"It's fun," Bess said. "You can even make one, too."

"Pretty grounds," Roxie noted as they walked.

"Oh, yes," Bess said and pointed out two new tennis courts, a clean-looking infirmary, a large baseball field and a white frame building which she said was the soon-to-be-completed new gym.

"And over there's the animal shelter, see? We have baby pigs and chickens and rabbits. Oh, and two baby goats. The kids take care of them—look, there's Hope. Hi, Hope!"

Hope waved and came toward them, with a group of tiny girls trailing after her.

"Roxie, what are you doing here?" Hope said with a grin. "Are you going to be working?"

"For the day, I guess," Roxie said. "I just came for a visit."

One of the little girls poked her fingers into Hope's tote bag and then quickly put her hands behind her back as Hope looked down.

"Now, Maryanne, you know those treats are for later. Y'all just keep your hands to yourself, hear?" Hope said and ruffled the girl's hair. "I have lollipops in there for them," Hope said. "Aren't they cute? They're just five . . . Girls, say hi to Roxie!"

"Hi, Roxie," the little girls chorused.

"Hi," Roxie said, smiling.

"Y'all know Bess," Hope said and the girls sang, "Hi" at Bess.

"We're going swimming," Hope said. "Maybe we'll see you at lunch time. Hope you enjoy your day, Roxie!"

Roxie watched the group trot off toward the lake. She started to say, "This isn't so bad," to Bess, but stopped herself when she realized how it would sound.

There were twelve molds for the ceramic plaques. Most were religious pictures of one form or another and two or three were short quotes from the Bible. The children poured clay into the molds, which were then baked by the counselors. When the hardened plaques came out of the kiln, the children painted and shellacked them.

"What if they want to make an ashtray?" Roxie whispered to Bess, who giggled.

"No one's supposed to smoke, silly," Bess answered. "But they can make little animals or something if they want. There are some other molds. The plaques are the most popular, though, because their mothers like to hang them in their kitchens to show them off."

The cabin smelled of turpentine and paint and fresh-cut wood, and seemed to Roxie a busy, happy place. Signs bearing single-word slogans were tacked up on all the walls: JOYFULNESS. TENDERHEARTED. CREATIVE. HONESTY. OBEDIENCE. CONTENTMENT. WISDOM. FAITH. DILIGENCE. All were lettered in bright-colored poster paints. The children, their faces, arms and legs covered with white chalky spots and streaks, chattered and laughed together as they worked. Roxie poured and baked clay, cleaned brushes, set out paints and found she was enjoying herself. When Bess had to leave to work in the office, Roxie decided to stay with crafts.

Hope's group of five-year-olds came in at one. Roxie took an instant liking to one child who wanted to sit in her lap.

"She's so cute," Roxie whispered to Hope. "She looks just like Annie! Remember that movie?" The little girl had a halo of golden-red curls and even wore a red sun-suit bordered in white.

Hope smiled sheepishly. "We don't go to the movies," she whispered back.

"Oh. Right," Roxie said and sighed.

"But I saw the posters," Hope added. "And I guess you're right . . ."

"Can I make a plaque, Roxie?" the child asked.

"Sure, honey. Go pick out a mold and bring it to me." Roxie watched the child trot over to the box where the molds were stacked. "What's her name?" she asked Hope.

"Diane Seeds. She's real poor, but she gets to come to camp 'cause her big brother's working on the new gym. Her sister, Molly, she goes to our school on scholarship. She's kind of wild . . . Anyway, I hope Diane grows up okay . . ."

"Roxie!" the crafts counselor called. "It's nearly one-thirty and you haven't had lunch yet! Why don't you run over to the dining hall and get something? Lunch may be over, but you tell them I sent you. You've been working like a little beaver!"

"Can I show her where it is?" little Diane begged. "Can I, Hope?"

"Sure. You come right back after, though, Diane . . ."

"I will, I will!"

Diane was so delighted with her chore Roxie didn't have the heart to tell her she already knew where the dining hall was.

"How old are you, Diane?" Roxie asked as they walked. Roxie walked; Diane skipped.

"Five-going-on-six!"

"You're a big girl. Do you like camp?"

"I love it!" She turned around and pointed. "See back there? That's my cabin. The second one in. And Hope's my counselor. She's nice—she gives us treats."

"What are those cabins over there?"

"Oh, those are the boys'. We can't go near there and they can't come near our cabins, either!"

"How come?"

"Because what if they *saw* us—" She put her hand over her mouth and giggled into it.

"What do you do at night?" Roxie asked. "After supper. Do you go right to sleep?"

"Sometimes. Or sometimes we have prayer meetings or group devotions or we see movies . . ."

"Movies? I thought you couldn't see movies."

"Oh, yes, we see movies. They're scary, too!" She made a hissing sound as she inhaled.

"Scary?"

"Uh-huh. One was about the Tribulations and this woman who wasn't saved got her head cut off! A man and his son got their heads cut off, too! I had bad dreams about it . . ."

I'll bet you did, Roxie thought and frowned.

"But *I'm* saved, though," Diane said confidently. "And my mama and my daddy and my brother and my sister are saved, too!"

"What are you saved from?" Roxie asked.

"Going to Hell," Diane answered. "This is the dining hall, but let's go in the back way—it's quicker!" She skipped ahead of Roxie, who was still frowning.

"Oh. The movies." Bess took a deep breath. "I know they seem scary to you, Roxie, and I guess they are. But they have to be. The children have to know what can happen to them . . . What *will* happen if they're not saved. The movies are *true,* the Tribulations will be *terrible,* so the children learn that no one who's saved will have to suffer them. And even though the stories may be frightening at first, afterward the children are relieved because they've turned to Jesus and they know no harm will come to them. Then they work hard to save others, you see. It's all there in Daniel and Revelation."

"What's being 'saved,' anyhow?" Roxie asked. "What do you have to *do* to get saved?"

"Roxie, it's so easy and so wonderful when it happens to you. And I pray that it does. Happen to *you,* I mean."

Roxie scratched at a mosquito bite.

"I really do pray for you, Roxie," Bess said again. "I think God sent you next door to us for a reason."

Roxie laughed. "Only if He's really named Harold Roper, who was my father's boss back in Syracuse and transferred him down here to Howerton."

"Don't blaspheme, Roxie," Bess said pleadingly, touching Roxie's arm. "I'm serious. God does have a purpose for everything."

Roxie sighed. "Well, tell me about being saved," she said. She didn't want to hurt Bess's feelings. Bess had, after all, been nothing but kind to Roxie from the first.

Bess's face seemed to glow. "All you have to do," she began, "is to relax. And just let Jesus come into your heart. You can say a little prayer, like 'Lord Jesus, I need You. Thank You for dying on the cross for my sins. Please take control of my life and do Your will through me . . . Make me the kind of person You want me to be . . .' Something like that. And then you've got to have faith that He'll come into your heart and be there forever . . . And then He does. He will!"

"Is it a real feeling then?" Roxie asked. "A real *knowing*, like your life has been changed?"

"Yes. And then you don't have to worry about anything ever again. God is in control from then on. If you worry about something, then you're just trying to do God's job for Him and that's not what He wants. It's *His* job to do the worrying and *you* have the peace. It's all in the Bible, Roxie. Just read Philippians!"

"You memorized the Bible?" Roxie asked incredulously.

"The Bible is the Word, Roxie," Bess said earnestly. "The answers are all there. We study the Bible and memorize passages and it helps because then you know just where to turn for guidance. You see, it's all right there at your finger tips."

Roxie looked over Bess's shoulder at the hills, purple against the sky. It's so beautiful, she thought. She looked down at the grass.

"I'm not trying to argue with you or anything, Bess," she said slowly. "It's just hard to think that you find answers to everything . . . in the Bible . . . that's all. I mean, it just seems . . . so simple!"

Bess beamed at her. "If you only knew how simple it is, Roxie! And even more important than the peace of mind you feel, is the personal relationship you have with Jesus. He's not someone far away, out of reach, but someone right inside your heart all the time!"

"How do you know?" Roxie asked. "How do you know He's with you—personally?"

"You just do. You focus on only the good things—

purity, honesty—you're out of the bad of the world and into only the good. And you know it."

"You feel it, Marian," Cynthia Preger was saying as they sat in the Cables' kitchen sipping Marian's special summer-fruit punch. "I mean, you *know* that pornography and crime and drugs—all those things keep on contributing to the breakdown of the traditional family, the destruction of America. Don't you?"

"Well, naturally I'm worried about the increase in—"

"Of course you are," Cynthia interrupted. "That's the point. Because instead of worrying, there are things you can actively do to stop it. We have to stop it, Marian, we have to stop the erosion of the family, the breakdown of moral purity, the—" She broke off and stood up quickly.

"Cynthia?" Marian asked.

Cynthia cleared her throat.

"Are you okay?"

"I'm fine." She sat down again. "I'm sorry . . . I get carried away sometimes . . . Mercy, I—" She cleared her throat again. "I'm fine, honey, really. What I was trying to say was just take a look at what the motto of today is: 'If it feels good, do it!' Now, do you see where that motto has got us? Look what the government wants to do: take your money, your taxes, and give it right away to lazy, indolent people who don't want to work, don't *have* to work, and why should they when they get handouts? Why should the government be allowed to do that with your very own hard-earned money?"

"Well, but someone has to help the poor, don't you think?" Marian said, leaning back in her chair.

"The church will help the truly indigent, Marian," Cynthia said, "not the government. 'Honor the Lord with thy substance, and with the firstfruits of all thine increase; so shall thy barns be filled with plenty, and thy presses shall burst out with new wine.' Proverbs, chapter three, verse nine. God will never let a right-thinking man starve."

Marian twisted uncomfortably in her chair. "Cynthia, I do admire your devotion, your strong faith—it's just that I guess I've never carried religion that *far* before . . ."

"Marian, that's just what I'm talking about." Cynthia reached out and touched Marian's hand. "With most people, religion is just something they think about on Sundays or at Christmas or Easter. It isn't a living, real part of their lives, and that's where it all goes wrong! I've had—I've known some . . . trouble . . . myself, and when I needed Jesus He was there. For me, Marian. He helped *me*. You see, you must have Jesus in your heart every second, sleeping or waking, and once you accept that, it isn't something you have to remember, it's a feeling and a faith that you have with you all the time to lean on. Dr. Caraman showed that to me, bless him."

"It sounds very"—Marian searched for the right word—"comforting," she said finally.

"Marian, I'm trying to make you see how all this isn't just aimless talk—how what I'm saying affects you. And Roxie. And your older daughter, too—Glenna?"

"Glenna, yes. How do you mean?"

"Don't you want to protect them from what's happening in the world? It's the young people, the hope of the future, I'm talking about. We want them to grow up right-thinking, not ready for the first temptation that steps in their way. Roxie's age—this is where it begins, Marian."

Marian touched her lips with her pinky thoughtfully.

"There's a girl right here in our town," Cynthia went on. "Well, there's more than one, of course, but the one I'm thinking of . . . Honestly, I pray for that family all the time."

"Why?"

"Well, just last spring, for example? She went skipping over to a house where this boy lives . . . At something like three in the morning. There she was, bold as brass, banging on his door, asking him to come out and take her somewhere. Just terrible, really. Everyone was talking about it. Lovely, polite God-fearing family, too, though the poor mama's not well. The girl's daddy got her into the academy with everyone's prayers that she'd turn around. I do believe she's all right now, thanks to Jesus. I just think about her poor family every day. I know the school and the church community's had a big effect on her—I can see it myself when she greets me and Joe . . . Jesus is in her heart now. I just wish—"

"Wish what, Cynthia?"

Cynthia patted Marian's arm. "Oh, honey, let's have some more of that delicious punch, all right? And I'll tell you all about some of the ministries I've been working in." She licked her lips and closed her eyes for a moment. When she spoke again, she almost whispered. "I just pray . . . that the Seeds girl's put all those worldly, sinful things right out of her mind, those awful television programs and sinful books and music . . ." She looked up at Marian. "We do have to be so careful about our children, don't we?"

V

In the weeks that followed, all three Cables were busy and productive. Roxie enjoyed working with the children at Camp Deliverance, and the days of sitting idly on her front porch with nothing to do seemed far away. Francis was happily absorbed in a new project for Arroway, and Marian began feeling better about herself, she decided, than she had in years. Shortly after her talk with Cynthia Preger, she joined the committee to help collect objects and furniture for the new Stafford Hill retirement home.

"It makes me feel needed," she told Francis when he mentioned how relaxed and happy she seemed. "Honestly, Frank, I'm busier than I've ever been, but oh, you should see the difference in that building!"

He smiled as she told him about wallpaper and end tables and a whole set of lovely china, with only one or two chipped pieces. She gave him a kiss as she filled his dinner plate with cold cuts.

*

One weekday, she found herself with a free morning. She wasn't due at the retirement home until one.

"I need a plan," she said aloud while she was dressing. "I need to stay active—it's good for the soul." And she laughed, thinking: I sound like Cynthia.

The smile stayed on her lips. She knew what she could do.

She hurried through a slap-together breakfast of coffee and a roll, then got into her car and drove to the Stafford Hill Baptist Church.

The parking lot was empty for a change and she pulled up next to the door of the main sanctuary.

Inside, the church was cool and still. The dark wood pews against the pale green carpeting made Marian think of meadows . . . clearings in forests . . .

Sanctuary.

Quietly, she slipped into a pew toward the front and leaned forward, staring at the altar.

Relax, Cynthia had told her. Open your heart and fill it with Jesus . . .

She sat in the same position for a long time. She didn't know how long. She didn't know if her heart was filled with Jesus but she did feel her restlessness leaving her and a sweet calmness taking its place. Finally, with a peaceful sigh, she stood and turned to leave.

"Hello there," a voice from the side said.

Marian, startled, drew in her breath. "Oh!" she said, "I didn't see you—"

The man came toward her. Smaller in stature than he appeared in the pulpit, he still seemed a person of great magnitude. He wore a dark suit, and a red tie. He gave

Marian a broad friendly grin as he held out his hand to her.

"Dr. Caraman . . ." Marian said, overwhelmed. She took the hand and his grip was hearty and warm. "It's a pleasure to—to meet you, to shake your hand!" She was afraid she was babbling. If she'd disagreed with some of his stands, she was still overcome with his presence: he was famous; he was forthright; his gaze was firm and penetrating but somehow comforting; and he was a man of God . . .

"I didn't want to disturb your prayers," he said, still gripping her hand, "but it's *my* pleasure, dear lady." He let go of her then and she felt her hand tremble. "Are you a visitor in our town?"

"No, I—we—my family and I, we've recently moved here. I've been—*we've* been to several services here and I've been working over at the retirement home. My daughter, Roseanne, she's—well, right now, she's out at Camp Deliverance. She's been working there pretty steadily with our next-door neighbor, Bess Preger—" Oh, dear, she thought, I'm just rattling on . . .

"The Pregers! Of course! Your name is—" He stopped for a moment, but held up his hand as she started to tell him. "Cable!"

"Yes," she managed.

"I know that your lovely daughter has been devoting her time to the children at Deliverance, though I haven't had the opportunity of meeting her yet. I know of your work, too, Mrs. Cable, and I'm filled with joy for you and your family, seeing your interests directed by Christ—in harmony with God's plan."

Marian smiled tentatively. "I so enjoy the work," she said, "and Roxie—Roseanne—does, too. In fact, I'm due over there—at the home, I mean—this afternoon. We're setting up the kitchen . . ."

"It's coming along beautifully," Clement Caraman said. "And I see in your eyes, Mrs. Cable, a woman whom I believe has been called to a holy life of service. I see you take joy and pleasure in allowing our Lord to work through you."

"Oh, I do—take pleasure—"

"Jesus takes pleasure in you, dear lady. This is why we're here, after all, isn't it? To bring delight to our Lord?"

Marian nodded.

"Come, sit down, Mrs. Cable," he said, sweeping his arm toward the nearest pew. "I rarely have an opportunity for a quiet time with individual church members—unless it's business, of course . . ." His voice trailed off in a chuckle.

"Oh, well—" Marian said as they both sat, "we haven't become members yet, but—"

"No?"

She felt a stab of guilt at the disappointment in his eyes.

"Well, not quite yet. But we have been thinking about it. Seriously," she added.

He smiled. "Have you accepted Jesus Christ as your personal savior?" he asked.

"I am a good Christian," Marian answered earnestly.

"I don't doubt that at all, dear lady. But when you ask Jesus to be your personal savior, you will know a life-changing religious experience. Do you believe that the Bible is the word of God and that it is a valid guide in all moral and ethical issues?"

"I—well, a guide, yes—" Marian thought, I'm stammering again. She felt as if she were a schoolgirl taking a test she desperately wanted to pass.

"Dear lady, I feel certain you are on the brink of a great discovery." He stood, forcing Marian to stand. Her legs wobbled. Again, he reached for her hand. "I know— I can see your family means a great deal to you."

"Oh, yes—"

"The family is sacred to the Lord. Traditional family values are the backbone of any nation. And we do want to preserve those values. Don't we, Mrs. Cable?"

"We do, yes . . ."

"I'll be seeing you again," he said, squeezing her hand even tighter, "I'm sure."

"Yes," she said, looking directly into his eyes. "I must tell you I'm grateful you—you've taken the time to chat with me like this—your busy schedule—"

"Let me say again that it's been my pleasure. Whenever I can I like to step in here or into the prayer chapel for a quiet moment of communion. And most happily, the Lord's purpose for me today was to see you here, too, and for us to meet and talk. Good day, Mrs. Cable. Please give my best to your family."

"I will. And thank you, Dr. Caraman . . ."

Was that a little bow? Marian thought as she watched him walk up the aisle. Was it really an old-fashioned bow or did I just imagine it?

*

Gradually, through the Pregers and through Marian's volunteer work, she and Francis found themselves invited to neighborhood potluck suppers. And the men invited Francis to watch baseball at their houses on the nights that their wives went to help with the mailing of the Stafford Hill Baptist Church bimonthly magazine, *Lifelight*.

When Marian returned one evening after helping with the mailing, she found her husband at home in front of the television set.

"I thought you were going over to the Hawleys' tonight," she said.

"I did for a while, but then I came back home." He snorted. "Their reception's just as lousy as ours. How was your evening?"

"Fine . . . You know, here we are becoming more active in this church and we still haven't joined yet," she said.

"You want to join?"

"I'm thinking about it . . . Do you think we should visit some others? Just to see what they're like?"

He yawned. "If you want . . ."

She shook her head. "I don't know . . . Everyone's so nice . . . I'm becoming more impressed with their concern for *families*. I do worry about Roxie, she's at such an impressionable age, Frank . . ."

"Tell you the truth, I'm more worried about Glenna, up there in New York all by herself," he said.

"Mmmm . . . Except she's not really all by herself. She does have Caroline . . ."

"That crazy roommate she found? I don't know, Marian . . . I guess you never stop worrying about your kids . . ."

"Well, Cynthia says that at this church and their schools they stress all the good values in life and the whole family works together to maintain them. You know, I'm worried about Roxie's going to Marble Avenue. I've heard there's a terrible drug problem there and lots of riding around in cars . . . This is an area where there isn't much for kids to do, so they get in trouble. At Stafford Hill, everyone's busy working."

"For the Lord," Francis added.

"Well, yes, but they're good causes, Frank. All those ministries for needy people . . . And Roxie certainly seems happier since she started working at their camp."

"Roxie likes little kids."

"I know . . . I just wish I could put these fears to rest. I really don't know what kind of school Marble Avenue is. We never saw it in session, Roxie and I. We just saw the building . . ."

"We'll find out soon enough," Francis told her. "I'm sure it's just like any other school. Like Dyer back home or any other . . ."

"I can't be so sure. Cynthia said she started her children in the public schools when they first moved here but pulled them out when she saw what they were like."

"Well, you know Cynthia. She can be a little extreme."

"I don't think she's being extreme in this case . . . Frank, can we turn off the television, please?"

"Sure." He rose quickly. He hated to see his wife upset. "You know," he said to soothe her, "I walked home with Joe Preger tonight. And he said some of those things . . . I thought, hey, I really can't fault the guy. Here we sit around in our living room and talk about the things that bother us, but Joe and Lew and the others—they really do something about them, with their letter campaigns and lobbying and all . . ." He gave Marian a quick hug. "Something to be said for that, eh, hon?"

"That's just what I was thinking," his wife answered.

On the last day of camp, Roxie, Bess and Hope, along with Hope's campers, got permission to take their lunches out of the dining hall and have a picnic on the lawn in back. They said grace, and as they began to eat, Hope turned to Roxie.

"Are our prayers going to be answered?" she asked.

"Which ones?" Roxie asked, smiling.

"The ones for you, silly. We pray for your eternal salvation. We want to win your soul, Roxie Cable."

"Thanks, kids," Roxie said.

"We're serious," Hope said.

"I know, I know. I like you both a lot and I appreciate what you're doing. I just . . . don't think that I can be committed the way you are," she told them.

"If you open your heart," Bess said, "you'll find a joy you've never known. You'll begin the great adventure for which God created you."

Roxie wished Bess wouldn't put it quite that way. It made her uncomfortable, and worse, it made her homesick for her friends in Syracuse who thought they'd begun their great adventure when they graduated from sixth grade. Bess was nice and sweet and she'd taught Roxie how to make a skirt on her sewing machine and how to make little animals by folding paper in special ways. Roxie appreciated Bess. But she could not appreciate her preaching.

"Okay," she said to lighten the mood, "but will you both still love me when I'm sixty-five?"

"Roxie, now you listen to Bess," Hope said, getting to her feet, "because she cares so much. It's fun to joke and kid around . . . But when it comes to winning souls for the Lord"—she touched Roxie's hair—"we really are serious. Now I've just got to get my little girls in for a swim before it's too late. Come on, y'all!" she called to her small campers, who began to gather their picnic things.

"Hope was right, Roxie," Bess said after Hope and her girls had hurried off. "And I'm going to tell you something even Hope doesn't know . . . because I think it might help you understand . . . just a little . . . about the workings of the Lord . . ."

Roxie frowned. "What?" she asked. "What do you mean?"

Bess pulled at a clump of grass. "I know we don't know each other all that well, Roxie," she said, "but I'd like you to promise me that you won't talk about this to anyone. Because it's awfully painful—to me, but especially to my parents. They never mention it at all."

"Bess, what is it?" Roxie asked, but still Bess hesitated.

"You understand that I'm telling this to you for your own sake and not for mine. Not for any sympathy, not for that reason . . . But because I want to show you what I've learned." Now she looked directly at Roxie as she played with the leaves of grass in her hand.

"It's all right, Bess, just tell me. Please," Roxie said, now anxious as well as curious.

"Well . . . You know I have an older sister . . ."

"Sure. Is this about Patty?"

"Well, no . . . Not exactly . . ." She took a deep breath. "Patty and I have a brother. *Had* a brother . . ."

"He's dead?" Roxie asked.

"Roxie, I don't even know whether he is or not, what do you think of that?" Bess smiled a sad little smile. It touched Roxie.

"What happened to him?" she asked.

Bess leaned forward, resting her chin on her hands.

"We moved here ten years ago," Bess said. "Did I tell you that? Patty was nine then and I was five. Joey— Joseph Junior—was thirteen."

"He was the oldest," Roxie said.

"Yes. We all enrolled in public school, it was all we thought of doing at the time. Like you," she added. Roxie didn't say anything. "Patty seemed to do all right in elementary school—she was only in the third grade. And I was just in kindergarten, but Joey went right into junior high school."

"Marble Avenue?"

"Yes. Well, it wasn't but halfway through the first se-mester that Mama and Daddy discovered Joey had been given drugs and was using them, using them regularly. And beginning to sell them, too."

"Oh, Bess—"

"Roxie, I'm sure Mama and Daddy don't know I know this much. I was so young when it happened . . . But there were so many fights and tears . . . Patty and I both knew. I didn't understand too much of it then, but I put it together later . . . because it went on a long time, you see. I got older . . ."

"How long?" Roxie asked. "What happened?"

"He promised he'd stopped. Those friends of his that none of us liked stopped coming to the house . . . I remember the times he promised he wasn't doing it any more . . . But then about a year later, Daddy discovered three hundred dollars stuffed behind a loose brick in the garage. Three—hundred—dollars, Roxie! Joey was only fifteen years old then!"

Roxie shivered. "He was still dealing . . . then . . ."

Bess was speaking quickly, running her sentences together. "You can't imagine how awful the battles were . . . I remember them so well . . . I guess I'll always remember them, but Roxie, we never talk about it. I think Mama would like to think it all got past me, but it didn't. None of it did. Patty, too. She used to cry herself to sleep at night and I used to hide under the bed . . ."

Roxie shivered even in the hot sun at the thought of a tiny Bess cowering under a bed, her hands over her ears . . .

"Finally, they sent Joey away to one of those halfway houses. You know, you must have heard of them. This one was in Texas. It nearly broke Mama's heart. All of us wrote, every single week. And we called him, too. Joey. He sounded better to me and Mama agreed, but Daddy said he'd sounded better before, too . . ."

"And anyway, one day, he disappeared."

"What?" Roxie's eyes widened.

"He just disappeared. He was supposed to be coming home. There wasn't enough money for him to fly, so Daddy said he'd drive all the way—to get him, you know? But Joey said no—by that time he was sixteen— and he said he wanted to travel himself. Said he'd take the bus. We never saw him after that."

"Bess!"

"He wasn't killed or lost, Roxie. He just ran away. I know because two months later there was a postcard. I was the one who brought it in from the mailbox outside. There was nothing written on it, not one word, but it was postmarked Denton, Texas. That's not too far from Dallas and Fort Worth . . . Patty and I looked it up . . ."

"Did your parents search—?"

"Oh, of course! Daddy did most of it and that was when he was trying to build the business, too. But there's not much hope, Roxie, when someone doesn't want to be found. That's what Mama said . . . They tried so hard to act cheerful around Patty and me, but when you live in the same house with people, you hear . . . Children hear . . ."

Roxie nodded.

"I missed Joey, but mostly I was so scared and upset for Mama and Daddy. Roxie, I just hated to hear my mama crying . . ."

Roxie swallowed.

"But I said there's a reason for my telling you this . . . didn't I?" Bess asked earnestly.

"Yes . . ."

"Do you know what happened after that?" Bess almost whispered.

"What?" Roxie asked quickly, wanting a happy ending.

"The Lord," Bess breathed.

"The Lord?"

"That's right. All of us—Mama, Daddy, Patty and I—we met and talked with Dr. Caraman. And what we learned, Roxie, was that the end result of all these harsh testings—no matter how harsh—can be a life of joy and dedication. Roxie, I don't know what would have happened to our family if we hadn't opened our hearts to Jesus!"

"Oh . . ."

"This is why I wanted you to know, Roxie, about Joey and about us. So that you could see, so that you could use what happened to our family and see what happens when you try to stand alone, outside the circle of a Christ-directed life. The world is wicked, Roxie, but we don't have to be doomed in it. And that's the service that we perform, you see—to protect the family unit, the children . . .

"Joey would be twenty-three now, wherever he is. And I pray every day for him. But I accept whatever is the Lord's will, and all will work out according to His plan."

Now Roxie looked away and began to pull at the grass.

"I'm so sorry, Bess," she said, "for everything you went through . . ."

"No, Roxie, I told you—it wasn't your sympathy I wanted!" Bess said quickly. "I want you to understand how much easier it is to accept life with all its trials and joys if you understand the reason we're put here on this earth. I don't want you to be damned, Roxie, I want you to be saved, *that's* why I shared the story with you. And Roxie . . . please promise you won't tell any-one—"

"Oh, I promise, Bess!"

"—because my parents never talk about it at all, and I think they'd be so upset if they knew that I—"

"I won't tell, Bess."

"We just don't remind them . . ." Bess said, looking off toward the mountains. "Even their friends who knew them then . . . But we all keep in our minds that there was a reason. And a plan. That's what I want you to keep in mind, Roxie. Because I'm your friend and be-cause I care."

VI

Roxie started school at Marble Avenue two weeks before Stafford Hill Christian Academy opened. She was nervous and excited the night before, but despite her fears, she somehow managed to find all her classrooms, and in time for the bell. That accomplished, she began to worry about never making any friends. No one paid her any attention. No one asked if she were new or where she came from or how she liked living in Howerton. Sometimes she had the feeling she was invisible.

The southern drawl she had gotten used to and even imitated unconsciously sounded suddenly strange in a classroom. She was fearful that teachers would call on her and fearful that they didn't know she existed. Unwilling to confide her worries to her parents, she wrote to her sister. Glenna's answer, by return mail, reassured her that all she was feeling was natural, that absolutely no one in a new place formed intimate friendships the first week and that she should relax and it would all work out. Roxie read and reread Glenna's letter, folded and refolded it and kept it with her in her purse.

"How was school today, dear?" her mother asked each day that week.

"Okay . . ."

"Just okay?"

"Uh-huh . . ."

"Do you have a lot of homework?" she asked on Friday night.

"Mmmm . . ."

"Did you meet anyone?"

Roxie shrugged. She remembered that Orrin Briley from the Pizza Hut had said he had a sister in tenth grade but Roxie hadn't heard the name Briley in any of her classes.

"Any nice girls in your classes?"

"I guess . . ."

"Do the kids seem . . . interested in their work? Is there a lot of . . . loitering around?"

Finally, Roxie made a face. "Moth-er . . ." she said. And Marian stopped.

When Roxie had gone up to do her homework, Marian complained to Francis.

"I can't seem to get her to talk to me," she said. "I want to know about the kids at Marble Avenue."

Francis didn't look up from the notes he was making on a yellow legal pad. "Well, you know how kids are, Marian . . . Roxie'll tell you the things that interest her, not the things that interest you . . ." He chuckled.

"I think we should join Stafford Hill, Frank . . ."

He put down his pencil. "Cynthia been at you again?" he asked.

"Oh, Cynthia asks me all the time. It's not Cynthia,

though. It's what it represents. The church, I mean. The values . . . You know . . ."

"I don't know, Marian . . ."

She faced him. "Why, Frank? What is it?"

"Well, I'm just not sure I like being told whom to vote for by a man from the pulpit. And I'm not at *all* sure I like the money I put in the collection plate going for purposes like that."

"But, Frank, that money goes for worthwhile things, too, like the retirement home, for example."

"Fine, but there sure is an awful lot of political pros-elytizing going on that I think you would have resented back in Syracuse—"

"Maybe," she interrupted. "Maybe so, but we're not back in Syracuse now and things are changing. The world is changing and we have a teen-age daughter to think about. I can overlook some of the things I may not like so much because I can see the whole picture: families—together—living good Christian lives, with good traditional values! There's nothing wrong with the traditional values, Frank."

"I never said there was, hon," he said with a sigh. "It's just that I'm not so sure I'm ready to overlook the things you're overlooking right now . . ."

"Try to think of it my way," she said, touching his arm. "Just try. Because I'm feeling afraid, Frank. And the merits of a church like Stafford Hill seem to out-weigh the offenses. They offer something to hang onto, something valuable. You said you can't argue with the values . . ."

"Okay," he said, picking up his pencil again. "But is

it all right if I get on with earning a living for a while? Meanwhile you can sing a little hymn for me to work by—"

"Oh, you!"

On the Monday morning of her second week at Marble Avenue, Roxie stopped in the hall to tie the plaid shoelace of her sneaker, causing a boy to trip over her foot. The boy bumped into another girl and both of them fell in a tangle next to Roxie.

Roxie rolled her eyes in mortification. Stumbling to her feet, she reached for books and papers. "Oh, gosh—here, let me help pick up your—oh, gee, I'm so—"

"Y'all sure picked a great place to make a sudden stop," the boy complained, brushing himself off. "Remind me not to go driving with you behind the wheel! Women!" he muttered and stomped off.

"What does being a woman have to do with it?" the other girl called after him. And when he didn't turn around: "You're a big turkey, DeWitt!" She faced Roxie with a wide grin. "I was going to say the same thing to you until he made that 'women' crack," she said.

Roxie smiled sheepishly. "I'm really sorry. You hurt?"

"Not a bit," the girl answered. "Lucky for you or I'd sue."

"Here's your notebook—" Roxie handed it to her. "I guess it was dumb to stop like that."

"Sure was, honey. Like to get yourself trampled to death when that bell rings and all the creatures get out of their cages. Where you from, anyway? No, don't tell me . . . Not Maryland, further north. Hmmmm . . .

New Jersey? No. New *York!* Somewhere in New York, right?"

Roxie laughed. "Syracuse, New York. How can you tell where someone's from?"

"Oh, it's just a game I play. I've got all the southern accents down pat. I can tell someone from Texas, South Carolina, Virginia, Alabama—everyone says, 'How can you do that, Mary Carol?' And I always say just from movies and television and records and just plain payin' attention! Anyway, I did live in Houston and Mobile for a while when I was just a bitty thing."

"Did you say your name was Mary Carol?" Roxie asked.

"Mary Carol Briley. Who're you?"

"Roxie. Roseanne Cable. I know your brother! His name's Orrin, right? And he works at the Pizza Hut?"

"Well, he did, but now he's away at college—the Woolcott Agricultural School?"

"Oh, well, I just met him once," Roxie explained, "when I had lunch there. He mentioned that he had a sister named Mary Carol—see, I'm new here and I don't know anyone, so I've been kind of listening for the one name I'd heard—well, anyway, it's nice to meet you."

"You're new here? Well, let lil' ol' Mary Carol show you some of that southern hospitality you probably read about but haven't seen. I am now your official ambassador to Marble Avenue High School, bless it's all-glass halls and pale blue blackboards. When's your lunch period?"

Roxie felt a knot loosening inside her. Mary Carol Briley sounded just like Ellie or Marge, only southern-style.

"Sixth," she answered.

"Well, I'm fifth," Mary Carol said, "but I've got study hall sixth, so I can eat with y'all anyway. And listen: don't buy it, *bring* it!"

They had lunch together that afternoon.

"Good thing you packed your own lunch," Mary Carol said. "Stuff this cafeteria serves is all starch. Bypasses your tummy and goes right to your hips. So you've been going to the Stafford Hill church, huh? How come?" She forked up some salad from a plastic container.

"My parents like it," Roxie told her. "My mother likes the church work. You know . . . helping people . . ."

"Pretty strict though, isn't it?"

Roxie shrugged.

"Did you get born again?"

"Huh?"

"Saved! Become a child of God! Received eternal life! You know, honey, taken into the arms of Jesus! Have you?"

Roxie was embarrassed. "We didn't join the church, we just . . . help out . . ."

"Mmmm," Mary Carol said. "Well, we belong to First Memorial. But we hardly ever go. Depends on the weather. Anyway, at least we can still go to movies and listen to rock 'n' roll and smoke. Stafford Hill doesn't let you do any of that, now does it?"

"I guess not," Roxie said. "But my parents really haven't restricted me or anything . . . There aren't even any movies around here to go to, anyway!"

"That's true, except over in Annenville," Mary Carol

said, "and that stuff's not exactly first-run most of the time . . ."

"I know lately my mother's been talking about the rising crime statistics and about drugs in the schools, but she hasn't said anything about movies or rock 'n' roll . . ." Roxie smiled. "What kind of stuff did you mean when you were talking about 'smoking'?"

"I meant cigarettes, honey," Mary Carol giggled. "But you can get pot if you want. You think *your* mother's harpin' on crime statistics? Honey, you should've heard mine when they opened up Willie Ketrick's locker last year and found a dime of pot in it! She'd like to of died! Grilled me for nearly an hour, but I told her no one ever tried to get *me* to use that stuff!"

"Did they?" Roxie asked.

"Sure!"

"Did *you?*"

"What, try smoking grass? Oh, sure. I mean, I'm not a head or anything. But sure, I've tried it. Haven't you?"

Roxie shook her head.

"I don't think you're missing anything, frankly. It just makes you hungry and who needs to gain weight!"

"Hi, neighbor," Cynthia called to Marian that afternoon over the small white fence that separated their houses.

"Oh, hi!" Marian called back. "Will you look at this garden? I started out so well and now it's just a mess."

"It's not a mess at all," Cynthia said. "And besides, you've been doing important work."

"Back home—" Marian began, then shook her head

impatiently, "I mean—back in Syracuse, I wouldn't be working on a flower garden in September. It's nice . . . how long the season lasts in the South."

"Well, it's all I've ever known," Cynthia said, "so I guess I don't give it much thought." She leaned against the fence and watched Marian work.

"Bess start school yet?" Marian asked. She was on all fours, tugging at a particularly stubborn weed.

"Mmmm, no. Wednesday. There's still time, Marian."

"For what?" Marian asked without looking up.

"Well, I was wondering if you were thinking any more about joining . . . The church and the school. For Roxie. I mean, the *school* for Roxie. The church for all of you . . . Have you, Marian?"

Marian sat back on the grass. "I have been thinking about it, Cynthia. I really have."

Cynthia spread her fingers across her chest. "I'm glad, honey," she said. "Bess and Joe and I talk about it so much—Bess prays Roxie'll be with her there at S.H.C.A. She's so fond of her, you know."

"Bess is sweet," Marian said. "Roxie's fond of her, too."

Cynthia nibbled at her thumbnail. "How's Roxie liking Marble Avenue?" she asked casually.

"We-ll, you know how it is with transplanted teenagers," Marian said. "She's a little lost still. But it's a new week. I guess she'll feel better when she makes some friends . . ."

"Roxie has loads of friends at Stafford Hill. And they're all just lovely, aren't they?"

Marian nodded. "They do seem like nice girls," she

agreed. "But I'm sure there are some nice young people at Marble, too . . ."

Cynthia lifted a forefinger. "I would watch the ones she meets, though, Marian. There's a peculiar element at that public school. At *all* public schools. You know, the trouble with modern education and modern psychology is that they encourage children to challenge their own parents. And according to the word of God, parents should have absolute authority over their children. Children in the public schools aren't taught that at all. And over at Marble Avenue—well, there doesn't seem to be *any* kind of discipline, if you know what I mean."

"What *do* you mean, Cynthia?" Marian asked, frowning.

"Only that I know those children don't do very worthwhile things with their leisure time . . . that trouble comes from 'idle hands' and all that? Honey, you just . . . watch the youngsters Roxie meets, now you do that." She rubbed her hand over a chipped place on the fence. "Isn't that awful? Now, Joe's been promising forever he'd repaint this ol' fence, it just looks terrible!"

Joe Preger owned a small printing firm in the town of Annenville, several miles north of Howerton. He had bought it from Cynthia's father shortly after they were married and he had built it steadily until it enabled him and Cynthia to buy their house on one of Howerton's prettiest residential streets. It was then and it is now, Joe thought—even prettier with all those young trees grown up.

"A good business, yessir," Joe whispered out loud as he sat at his desk. It had gotten them through the trouble and then it had helped get the girls out of the public school and into the academy. The business. Joe really loved it. It was like another— He thought of the word, *child,* but put it out of his mind quickly. Not like that— more like a friend. Like a friend.

But now . . .

He rubbed his eyes with his fingers, brooding. The economy, he thought, was almost as bad as when he first bought the company. But then, of course, he was young, he was ambitious, he had nowhere to go but up . . . He grunted aloud.

This year, he thought, shaking his head . . . So bad. People were using the same promotional material they'd used before, ordering no new brochures and bringing advertising revenue way down.

He'd already taken out a loan for Patty's college and hadn't told Cynthia. He knew she'd just worry. He had been able to pay for Bess's school but he wondered how long he could continue to afford it.

Joe stood up, admitting to himself finally that he had nothing more to do that day. He looked at his clean desk. "I hate clean desks!" he said aloud and walked outside.

He choked back a sob of frustration when his car wouldn't start, then took a deep breath and leaned heavily against the back seat.

"Jesus, forgive me," he whispered with his eyes closed. " 'Yet it pleased the Lord to bruise him; He hath put him to grief; when thou shalt make his soul an offering for sin, he shall see his seed, he shall prolong his days, and the pleasure of the Lord shall prosper in his hand. He shall see of the travail of his soul and shall be satisfied' . . ."

Joe breathed deeply again. "I'm sorry, Lord. Forgive me for not rejoicing in this test You have given me."

He tried the engine once more, then got out and went back into his office, where he picked up the phone.

"Frank? Joe. Listen, you about through for the day? Because I've got engine trouble here and I was wondering if you could pick me up on your way home . . . Great. I'll call the garage and be out front when y'all come by. Thanks, Francis . . ."

"They pick your car up?" Francis asked as Joe slid in to the front seat beside him.

"Yep. Thanks a lot for this, Frank . . ."

"It's nothing, don't mention it. I'll give you a lift in the morning, too."

"Aw, great."

They sat in silence for a while. Then Francis asked casually, "How's the independent businessman doing these days?"

"Oh! Fine!" Joe said heartily. Then: "I'm lyin', Frank. It's really not so good."

Francis, struck by his serious tone, turned to him. "Gee . . . I'm sorry to hear that, Joe."

"I'll be okay, I'll be okay . . . Hard, though. Well, Hebrews tells us that these trials are 'for our profit, that we might be partakers of His holiness,' right, Frank?"

"If you say so, Joe . . ."

"Now, Francis, you need to have more faith . . ." He suddenly put his face in his hands. Francis noticed the redness around his ears.

"Joe? Hey, Joe . . ."

"I'm all right, Frank. Momentary bad spot there . . . I'm really all right." He turned his face to the window. "There was a time, Frank . . . A very bad time for me . . . and Cynthia . . . Kids can be—can be so—well, but coming to know God changed everything for us, I just can't tell you, Frank . . . Once you know and experience God's love, His plan for your life . . . Well . . ." He turned to face Francis. "Be happy you have two wonderful daughters, Frank. Be glad. Protect them, Frank . . ."

"Well, I am glad, Joe. I am. But you have two fine girls yourself there."

"Yes. Yes, I do."

That night at dinner, Roxie felt a definite shift in moods. It was she who was talkative and bubbly, while her mother and father seemed thoughtful, far away.

". . . And isn't it nice," she was saying, "that I did meet her after all and she turned out to be fun? We have the same gym class!"

"Who?" Francis asked.

Roxie frowned. "I just told you, Daddy. Mary Carol Briley! This new girl I met at school. Well, I mean *she's* not new, *I'm* the new one, but she's new to me, anyway . . ."

"I'm glad you made a friend, honey," her father said absently.

"What's she like, Roxie?" Marian asked.

"I told you, she's nice. She's fun. She can tell where you're from by your accent!"

Marian picked up her knife and fork and put them down again.

"Yes, but what's she *like*? Is she like Ellie or any of your other friends from Syracuse? What I mean is, is she a nice girl or a . . ."

"A what?" Roxie asked.

Marian exhaled. "I don't know exactly what I'm trying to say. Mrs. Preger was talking today about a bad element over at Marble Avenue. You know, kids who use drugs. Things like that. She worried me a little."

"Oh, Mom, there're always drugs available. There were at Dyer, too. Everybody knows that. Mary Carol said you could get drugs if you want."

"She did?" Marian's eyebrows shot up.

"Yes, Mo-ther," Roxie said, as if she were talking to a child. "But that happens anywhere, it's just a fact of life!"

"Does Mary Carol use drugs?" Marian asked, trying to sound casual.

"Well, she's *tried* pot . . . I mean, who hasn't?" Roxie answered defensively.

"*You* haven't," Marian said, leaning toward her. "Have you?"

"No! Honestly, Mother, she only tried it. Millions of kids try it, it doesn't mean they're 'drug users'!"

"Change your tone, Roseanne," Marian cautioned.

"I'm sorry," Roxie said quickly. "But you know what

I mean. I'm not talking about kids who sit stoned through all their classes!"

Marian frowned.

"Come on, Mom, you can't escape things like that. Did you worry when Glenna was in school, too?"

"Yes," Marian answered thoughtfully, "sure I worried about Glenna . . . but . . . I don't know, I guess I felt safer then. I mean, I knew the whole neighborhood, knew all the kids Glenna went to school with . . ." She paused. "I don't know, it just seemed there wasn't anything I could do back then. I didn't think I could make a difference . . . back . . . then . . ." She stopped again, trying to collect her thoughts. Then: "Francis, you haven't said one word! What do *you* think?"

His plate was still full. He'd hardly touched a bite.

"Uh, about what?" He pulled himself up when he saw the expression on his wife's face. "I'm sorry, I was only half listening . . . You mean about drugs in the school? Was that it?"

"Mom worries more about me than she did about Glenna," Roxie said teasingly. "I just mentioned that someone I knew had tried marijuana so she thinks I'm in with the druggies. I bet Glenna never even mentioned the kids she knew who smoked and drank, so Mom didn't worry. I just thought she knew it was a plain old fact of life!"

"It isn't just the drugs," Marian said. "It's the downward road we seem to be headed on these days. And this is a town where there isn't very much to keep the young people occupied. They get bored, and that's when there's trouble."

Francis rubbed his eyes. "I suppose," he said, "that we'll

have to wait a while and see how things shape up for Rox. It's all we can do, isn't it?"

Marian sighed. "I suppose . . ."

"I'll clear and do the dishes by myself tonight," Roxie said, standing up. "Okay?"

"Don't you have homework?" her mother asked.

"Uh-huh, but I'll still have lots of time to do it . . ." she said, stacking their plates.

As she disappeared into the kitchen, Marian looked over at her husband.

"You hardly ate a thing," she said.

"Mm."

"What is it, Frank? Everything all right at work? You're so distracted . . ."

He stretched and reached for the coffee pot on its trivet.

"Nothing, really," he told her. "I told you I brought Joe home tonight . . ."

"Yes, his car died . . ."

"Yeah . . . I guess I was thinking about him. His business isn't that good, seems he has money worries . . ."

"Familiar story," Marian said.

"I know, but—I guess he had some family trouble a while back, at least that's what he intimated."

"I think you're right. I got a hint of that from Cynthia, too. But it certainly isn't true now. They're a lovely family. Their faith seems to help them enormously."

Francis nodded slowly. "Guess so. Got a glimpse today of how much it means to Joe, but I just don't know about me . . . Say listen, hon, what do you say we give Glen a call tonight? Just to say hello."

*

"Can you go to a party?" Mary Carol asked Roxie one week in late September. "It's Friday night. Do you know Emily Biggers?"

"Uh-uh."

"Well, it doesn't matter. Emily won't care if I bring a friend. Bobbie's going, Bobbie Sue Overmeyer? She's that friend of mine in your English class—"

"Right . . ."

"And there'll be some eleventh- and twelfth-grade boys. Nice kids. You'll like 'em."

"Sure, I can go," Roxie said. "I'm not doing anything special Friday night."

"There'll be rock 'n' *roll,* you know . . ."

"I told you, we didn't join Stafford Hill, Mary Carol . . ."

"I know, Roxie, I'm just teasing. But your mama won't be mad or anything, will she?"

For an answer, Roxie poked her finger in Mary Carol's ribs.

"Where is the party?" Marian Cable wanted to know.

"At a friend of Mary Carol's. Emily Biggers. I don't know where she lives yet. I'll find out. I told her I'd go . . ."

"Roxie, you should have asked first," her father said.

"Well, gee, we're not doing anything. Why did I have to ask?"

"I would appreciate it if you would check with us first before you make any commitments," Marian said.

"Mom, I think you said that with a southern accent,"

Roxie said. "You're getting to sound like Mrs. Preger."

"Roxie—"

"Oh, don't get mad. It's just that you didn't say things like that to me back in Syracuse. If I said I was going to a party on a weekend or something, you just said, 'Have a nice time.' "

"We felt we knew the area, Rox," her father said, "and all the kids, that's all."

"Will this Biggers girl's parents be home?" Marian asked.

Roxie said, "Sure."

"You don't know that for sure, Roxie, now do you?"

"Oh, Mother, why did you ask me then, if you don't believe my answer!" Stalking out of the room, Roxie heard her mother call, "I want you to make sure that someone will be at home during the party or I will not let you go!"

"Did she answer? I couldn't hear," Francis said when Roxie had left the room.

"I don't think so." Marian sighed. "Lately she keeps leaving the room in a huff each time we talk. I don't know what to do with her."

"It's the age," Francis said.

"Oh, maybe . . . Am I wrong to want a parent home when my fifteen-year-old goes to a party? Is anything wrong with that?"

"No, hon, of course not . . ."

Marian sat thoughtfully for a while.

"I wonder if they'll be playing that awful hard-rock music," she said.

Francis smiled. "Now you *do* sound like Cynthia Preger," he said.

"Well, I do agree with her that that kind of music isn't exactly uplifting for the soul . . ."

"It's not the music I object to," Francis said, "so much as maybe other things that can go on. You know . . ."

"Dr. Caraman says that we'll only triumph by not conforming to the standards of a sinful society. He says with a strong faith we learn to concentrate on the pure and good . . ."

"Look, hon," Francis said, "I think it's probably best to go kind of slow with Rox. She hasn't exactly been overwhelmed by the words of the great Clement Caraman yet . . ."

"It isn't Dr. Caraman!" Marian blurted and then reddened at her husband's smile. "It isn't, Francis. I know what you mean about some of the extremes, some of the things he espouses . . . But so much of what he says makes sense to me. And you were the one who pointed out that Stafford Hill people and others like them are the ones who accomplish things, while the liberals sit around discussing them, right? Didn't you?"

"I did, I did . . ."

"And didn't you mention how Joe Preger's faith got him through?"

"Yes . . ."

"Well, I like that, Francis," she said vehemently. "I want that for us. I want to feel that Roxie's growing up safe in an uncertain world and that I can make a difference in that world if I work and try and believe. And I'd like to feel that Glenna's safe in the world, no matter how far away from us she is. Don't you want that too, Frank?"

*

Emily Biggers' parents did insist on staying home the Friday night of their daughter's party, but Emily had extracted a bargain from them that they would never appear below the first step leading to the basement.

"But I can't see anything from the first step," Mrs. Biggers complained, to which Emily replied that there would be nothing to see, that she and her friends deserved privacy and that her parents would still be within hearing distance of everything if they remained in the kitchen, "which I certainly hope you don't do," Emily sniffed. "I should think y'all'd want to go to bed instead of listening to a lot of boring kids dancing to music you hate!"

After only an hour of sitting on a kitchen chair directly above the record player, Mr. Biggers was ready to call it a night and Mrs. Biggers, overwhelmed by the amount of potato chips, pretzels, Cheetos, Fritos, crackers, cheese, lemonade, iced tea and pop consumed in sixty short minutes, beat her husband to the stairs, fanning herself with the Howerton *Sun & Chronicle*.

Roxie danced with a boy named Arthur, who had come to the party from Annenville with two friends, and with another boy whose name she didn't catch, and who also didn't have a very good sense of rhythm.

She enjoyed herself nevertheless, because Mary Carol was especially funny describing people and because she never felt alone, the way new people usually do in strange places. Emily Biggers was warm and friendly, and her guests seemed genuinely interested in meeting Roxie.

"It's a nice party," she said to Emily, who was walking by with a bowl of peanuts. "Thanks for letting me come with Mary Carol."

"Any friend of Mary Carol's is a friend of mine," Emily sang at her. "Anyway, the party's okay, but it'll get better." She moved closer to Roxie. "The loud music's designed to fumigate parents. After they go to bed we can relax . . ."

By relaxing, Emily meant that several six packs of beer could be brought out from a cooler in the back of someone's car, and that two carefully rolled joints of marijuana could be passed around to anyone wishing to partake.

"Y'all want a toke, Roxie?" Mary Carol drawled. "I don't. I can't even have any beer . . . It's too fattening."

"No," Roxie said.

"Emily has these parties because that way she gets free pot," Mary Carol said. "Her parents buy the food and supply the house, so she has no overhead, know what I mean? But she's fun, Emily is, don't you think?"

"Yeah," Roxie agreed.

"Uh-oh," Mary Carol said, looking across the room out of a corner of her eye, "there they go again . . ."

"Who? What?"

"Don't look, but back there—I said don't look!" Mary Carol said. "It's Annie and Conway, they just can't keep their hands off each other. Look what he's doing—no, don't!"

Roxie laughed. "Can I look or not?"

"Don't look. I'll tell you. Well, he's got his hand right smack down the front of her blouse. Wouldn't you think they'd go upstairs or something?"

"Who are they?" Roxie asked.

"Oh, Annie's a junior and Conway's a senior. They've

been going together since last year. I mean, myself, I just love to see people in love, but I get real squiggly when they practically *do it* right out in public, don't you?"

"Maybe I would if I could see it," Roxie said, peering over Mary Carol's shoulder.

"Oh, I guess it's okay for you to look. They never have cared who saw them, I'm sure. Ooooh, would you look at that kiss? Well, at least they're dancing, so they have an excuse to wrap themselves around each other like that."

"Yes, but it's not slow music," Roxie said, smiling.

"Now what possible difference could the music make?" Mary Carol laughed. "Roxie, when you have a boyfriend, do you think you'd make out in front of the world like that?"

"No," Roxie said, blushing, "I don't think so . . ."

"Me, neither, but I think I'd like the opportunity to find out . . ." She rolled her eyes. "Same old faces here, so I don't think I'll meet my special boyfriend tonight! Oh, well . . . How about some sugarless iced tea?"

Emily Biggers' parents, as promised, did not appear below the first step of the basement stairs. But Roxie's father, coming to pick her up at eleven-thirty, did.

The party was just beginning to break up at that time and Roxie didn't see Francis until she turned toward the stairs to watch the way Annie and Conway would negotiate the climb with both their arms still around each other.

"Daddy!" Roxie cried, surprised. Then, to Mary Carol: "Is it eleven-thirty already?"

"Uh-huh. Is that your father up there? He's cute, Roxie."

Roxie saw her father frown as Conway bumped against him.

"I don't think he *feels* cute," she whispered. "I have to go. Do you want a lift home?"

"No, thanks, my daddy's coming for me pretty soon, if he can yank himself away from the bowling alley. Y'all go on, honey, I'll see you Monday in school."

"That was a very romantic couple I saw leaving the party," Francis said to Roxie in the car.

"I knew you'd say something about that . . ."

"You knew I'd say something about that?" Francis repeated.

"Well, you just looked kind of—disapproving," Roxie said.

Her father frowned. "Well . . . it wasn't just . . ." he began and stopped. "How was the party? Did you have a good time?"

"Pretty good. Mary Carol is really fun to be with. Emily's nice . . . I danced with a couple of guys . . . Yeah, I guess I liked it."

"I noticed some beer cans."

"Yeah, some kids brought some in . . ."

"And I didn't see any parents around. In fact, no one answered my knock. I came in and found the basement all by myself."

"Emily's parents were there," Roxie said. "But they went to bed after a while."

"That's not much chaperoning," Francis said. "Did they know there was beer?"

"I don't know, Daddy . . ."

"And I saw a little group on the floor who looked pretty out of it," he added.

"Daddy, gosh . . . What is this, a third degree?" Roxie asked defensively. "I had a nice time, didn't have any beer . . . Don't you trust me?"

He reached over and patted her leg. "Of course I trust you, Rox. I just think it's hard when you're young and exposed to all kinds of temptations . . ."

"It's not hard. I didn't *want* any beer. I didn't *want* any grass, so I—"

"There was marijuana, too?" Francis asked, taking his eyes from the road and looking at Roxie.

"Daddy, look where you're driving."

"Don't tell me how to drive, young lady. Now you tell me: just what *else* was going on at that party?"

He slammed the bedroom door, startling his wife, who had been sitting up in bed, reading.

"Frank, what—?"

"Beer, marijuana, necking . . ." he mumbled.

"What?"

"Some party, some party. I don't remember anything like this with Glenna . . ."

Marian took off her glasses. "Is Roxie all right?"

"Yes, she's fine, but I don't know how long she'll be fine."

"Oh, Frank . . ."

"We'll do it," he said, smacking his palm against the bedpost. "Let's do it, let's join Stafford Hill. Sunday. Right after the service!"

VII

On the following Sunday morning, the Cables and the Pregers went to services at the Stafford Hill Baptist Church together. Roxie and Bess sat next to each other, with Cynthia and Marian in the middle and Joe and Francis at the other end, on the aisle. Throughout the service, Cynthia took Marian's hand with a wam squeeze or touched her arm and smiled. Marian returned the squeeze and the smile and felt a tiny thrill rush from her chest to the pit of her stomach. By the close of the service, she had begun to tremble.

"We'd like to take time now for anyone," Clement Caraman said in the echo of the final hymn, *"anyone,* who has a problem, a need, or who wishes to join Stafford Hill or who wants to start a church . . . We'd like to take time now to have that person, those persons, come down the aisles now, right here—where one of our pastors will take you into a prayer room for quiet talk. Please . . . Don't be afraid or embarrassed. We want you to come down here right now."

The organ continued to play softly and the secondary

pastors of the church lined up in a row at the front to receive those who had begun their walk forward.

"*Now,* Marian," Cynthia whispered, stepping back to let Marian pass in front of her. "Go ahead . . ."

"I can't, my legs feel like water," Marian whispered back.

"Come on, honey. Look, Francis is waiting for you in the aisle . . ."

Marian looked toward her husband, who was standing next to their pew with his hand out, ready to take hers as she came to him.

"All right, I'm ready," Marian said, and murmured over her shoulder, "Come on, Roxie, . . ." as she inched past Cynthia and Joe.

Roxie bit her lip and didn't move.

Cynthia moved next to her. "Go on, Roxie, honey. The whole family should go together."

"It's all right," Roxie said, so softly that Cynthia had to strain to hear her. "I'd rather have the adults handle it themselves."

"Honey, don't be embarrassed. It's a lovely thing when the entire family goes together to join the church. Come on, there's still time to catch up . . ."

But Roxie hung back.

"N-no, I don't like to do the talking," she said. "Mom and Dad can join for me . . . The family's joining . . . I just don't want to—have to . . ." She shrugged and smiled sheepishly.

Cynthia smiled and put an arm around Roxie's shoulders. "All right, honey. You'll get over being embarrassed now that Jesus has entered your heart forever." She leaned close to Roxie. "I have prayed for just this moment, Roxie, dear," she said. "And so has Bess. Haven't you, Bess?"

Bess nodded, her face flushed. "I'm real, real happy for you, Roxie," Bess said.

"And we've planned a lovely luncheon to celebrate this happy occasion, your planting your feet on the road to a successful life with Jesus as your personal savior. 'Suffer the little children to come unto me, and forbid them not: for of such is the kingdom of God.' "

"Welcome, Roxie," Bess said, and leaned over and kissed Roxie's cheek.

The three girls got off the Marble Avenue bus giggling and pushing each other lightly as they chattered.

"He is *too* the cutest," Mary Carol insisted as Roxie made a face. "He is, too, isn't he, Bobbie?"

The third girl nodded enthusiastically. "I just love his eyes, don't you? They are so *blue!*"

"That's probably why he went into teaching," Roxie said, grinning. "—to watch all the young girls drool over him. I don't think he's so cute . . ." She pointed. "That's my house. We have to cross the street."

The other two followed her as she stepped off the curb.

"Well, who do you think is cute, then?" Mary Carol asked. "I mean, if you don't think Mr. *Brad*-ley is gorgeous, who *is,* I'd like to know?"

"Kermit the Frog," Roxie said, climbing the steps to her front porch. "Now, that's *cute!*"

Mary Carol gave Roxie another teasing push as Marian opened the front door to greet them.

"Hi, Mom," Roxie said. "What are you doing home? I thought you were, uh, going to be out all afternoon."

"Well, I was," Marian said, eyeing the two strangers, "but I had to stay here until the man came to fix the dryer . . . so we decided to go tomorrow . . . Aren't you going to introduce me to your friends?" She smiled hesitantly.

"Oh! Sure! This is Mary Carol Briley. Remember we met her brother at the Pizza Hut? And this is Bobbie Sue Overmeyer . . . This is my mother."

Bobbie said, "How do you do, ma'am?" and Mary Carol said, "S'nice to meet you, Mrs. Cable."

"Hello, girls . . . Well, please come in. Come in," Marian invited, stepping away from the door. "I guess you girls are in the same class?"

"Yes, Mother, this is Mary *Carol*," Roxie said, silently adding, I've mentioned her a thousand times, "and Bobbie is in my English class."

"You went to a party together . . ." Marian said.

"Yes . . ." Roxie said, looking away. She'd heard enough of her parents' views on Emily's party and didn't want the girls to hear them. But suddenly, Cynthia Preger appeared in the kitchen door.

"Well, hello there, Roxie," Cynthia said.

"Hello, Mrs. Preger . . ."

Cynthia nodded curtly to Roxie's friends and turned to Marian.

"Honey, have you ever heard of Dr. Lawrence Weaver?" she asked. "No? Well, he's a great preacher from Tennessee, he has that TV show, 'Bear Witness to the Light'? Well, anyway I thought I'd add his name to

the list of guest preachers we thought of inviting . . .
He's a very stirring speaker. I've seen him . . . What do
you think?"

Roxie shifted her weight from one foot to the other
as Marian told Cynthia she thought Dr. Lawrence
Weaver sounded just fine to her.

"We're going to go upstairs, okay?" Roxie said, moving out of the living room. She had intended to offer
the girls a snack in the kitchen first, but it was obvious
that her mother and Cynthia were at work in there.

"All right . . ." Marian said, watching them leave.

". . . And we can just split up this list and you call
the top half and I'll call the bottom," Cynthia was saying.

Roxie closed her door quickly behind the two girls.

"Your mama does church work?" Bobbie said, flop-
ping onto the floor.

"Mmm-hmm," Roxie said.

"You joined, huh?" Mary Carol asked. A corner of
her mouth turned up.

"Mmm," Roxie said noncommittally.

"Joined what?" Bobbie asked.

Mary Carol rolled her eyes. "Stafford Hill," she answered.

"Really?"

"Oh, it's just a church," Roxie said. "My mother likes
the work."

"It's more than a church," Mary Carol said as she sat
on the edge of Roxie's bed. "It's a whole way of life.
We know a lot of kids who belong, don't we, Bobbie?
I really feel sorry for them."

"Oh, come on," Roxie said feebly.

"It's just real strict is all," Bobbie said. "But at least you go to public school, Roxie. You get to mix with us sinners, so you can see the interesting side of life! Only don't try to win *my* soul, honey-lamb!" She laughed and rolled over on her stomach. "Oh, records!" she cried as she noticed Roxie's collection on the bottom shelf of a wall unit.

"What've you got?" Mary Carol asked, bouncing off the bed. She and Bobbie flipped through the albums, murmuring excitedly.

"Oooh, these are good, you have *all* of The Dead?" Bobbie cried.

"Not all . . ." Roxie said. She slid over on the floor to join them. "A lot of these are my sister's. See, look, there's 'Some Girls' by The Stones!"

"I know that!" Bobbie squealed. "Let's put it on!"

They had to yell at each other to be heard over the music but that didn't bother any of them.

"Isn't this illegal or something?" Mary Carol asked. "You can't listen to rock 'n' roll if you're a Stafford Hill member!"

Roxie said, "Come on, let's talk about something besides church!"

"Can you go on a date without a chaperone?" Bobbie asked.

"Will you stop it?" Roxie said it teasingly but she was getting annoyed.

"I'm serious. Can you?"

"She can go anywhere with Kermit the Frog!" Mary Carol said, making them all laugh again until the door opened suddenly and they looked up to see Marian with Bess Preger. The girls on the floor fell silent but the music blared on.

"Turn that down, Roxie," Marian said, and Roxie quickly lifted the needle.

"My goodness, that's better," Marian sighed. "That was much too loud, dear." And then she added, "Bess is here."

"Hi, Bess," Roxie said. "This is Mary Carol and Bobbie."

"I know Bess," Bobbie said. "Hi . . ."

Bess said, "Hello."

"Well, I'll get back to my work," Marian said, and went out, leaving the door open.

Now the room was silent, except for the hum of the spinning turntable.

"How're you, Bess?" Bobbie asked politely.

"Just fine . . . Your daddy all right, Bobbie Sue?"

"Oh, yes, he's back at work and ever'thing . . ."

"That's nice . . ." Bess turned to Roxie. "We were witnessing over at the hospital last spring and Bobbie Sue's daddy was there," she explained.

"He fell off a ladder," Bobbie added. "Broke his leg and his other ankle. But he's just fine now . . ." Her voice trailed off.

"Would you like something to eat?" Roxie asked, jumping to her feet. "I'll bring some stuff up from the kitchen!"

"Listen, no, it's okay, honey," Mary Carol said, and also stood. "I think Bobbie and I better get on home . . ."

"Oh, no—"

"Really, we ought to go," Bobbie said. "I have to pick up my little brother at day care anyway."

"Do you have to leave so soon?" Roxie asked. "And how will you get home?"

"We'll just catch the bus on the corner," Mary Carol said.

"I'll be back to hear the rest of your—um—" Bobbie stopped in midsentence. "Well . . . We'll see you, Roxie . . ." she said instead.

"I'll walk you down," Roxie answered, moving past Bess. She hurried to keep up with the girls on the stairs.

"Listen," she said, "do you really have to go now? Couldn't you stay a little longer? I mean, Bess won't— she didn't mean—"

"No, Roxie, honest," Bobbie said, "my mama'd be furious if I didn't get my brother on time."

"We'll see you tomorrow in school," Mary Carol said at the door. "And thanks, Roxie."

What for? Roxie wondered as she let them out. She was already dreading the thought of school tomorrow.

Bess was studying the record albums when Roxie reentered the room.

"Are they illegal?" Roxie asked, facetiously repeating Mary Carol's question.

"No, they're not illegal, Roxie, it's just that when you let worldly things control your life, then your life is not controlled by the Holy Spirit, as it's meant to be. Romans, chapter twelve, verse two: 'And be not conformed to this world: but be ye transformed by the renewing of your mind, that ye may prove what is that good, and acceptable, and perfect will of God.' You must discipline yourself to give up things that are an obstacle to that perfection, to that moral goodness and purity."

Roxie sighed. She wished she were as sure as Bess that the Bible was the answer to everything.

"It's just music, Bess . . . It's not controlling my life," Roxie said.

"It's a step, Roxie. It's just a step downward instead of in the direction of righteousness. Oh, honey—" She put down the album she was holding. "I'm just trying to help, to be your friend. Those girls—if I make them uncomfortable . . . I think they respect the strength that I have in my belief. I don't *need* what they need to be happy inside myself, do you see? I want that for you, too, Roxie. I really do like you and I do believe you have so much to offer in service."

"Your friends left without saying goodbye," Marian said later when she and Roxie were alone.

"Well, you were in the kitchen. They didn't want to disturb you."

"They left practically as soon as Bess walked through the door. Why was that?"

"Because Bess makes them feel uncomfortable, that's why," Roxie answered. "Why did you bring her up? I didn't invite her."

"Roseanne, now what was I to do, when she came over and asked to see you? Her mother was here . . . What was I supposed to—"

"Okay, I'm sorry," Roxie said. "Bess is nice, but she doesn't mix with the Marble Avenue kids, that's all. She acts like she's better than they are."

"I don't think that's true," Marian said. "And Bess was polite enough to seek me out and say goodbye before she left. I think your friends might have been kinder to Bess and not walked out the minute she arrived. I do think that was rude, Roxie. I'm sorry but I do."

"Well, I just hope," Roxie said, "that they weren't scared off from coming back here, that's all!" She stomped upstairs to her room.

At school, Roxie watched carefully for any signs of standoffishness in Mary Carol but was happy to see that her friend was as warm as ever.

"Don't worry about it, Pious Polly," Mary Carol teased. "It wasn't you. Bess Preger gives Bobbie a pain— she has ever since they met at the hospital last year. There was poor Bobbie Sue's daddy, lying there with his legs swingin' up practically over his head, and Bess and her big sister and some of those others are carryin' on, tryin' to bring him to Jesus when all he wanted was another shot of Demerol. Don't you worry, honey, you just turn up The Stones real loud when you figure you've gotten a little too much of Bess Preger and you'll be all right!"

Clement Caraman smiled as his guest speaker left the pulpit and sat down in a chair directly in front of the choir. The church rang with the applause of thousands in the pews. Caraman waved his hand, encouraging the applause.

"Of course, it's fine to applaud!" he cried. "This wonderful ballplayer, whom you've seen many-a-time turning over the key double play in the late innings of a close game—this man, known all over our great country as the league's foremost second baseman, has seen fit to come all the way down here to Howerton to give his personal testimony at our Sunday service today!" He joined the renewed applause. "Thank you, Bill—we *all* thank you! You're leaving with our gratitude and heart-felt prayers!"

Joe Preger leaned over toward Francis. "Wasn't that moving!" he whispered. Francis nodded.

The baseball player stood, shook hands with Clement Caraman and quietly left through a door leading to the offices in the back. Once more, the church was silent.

"One of the things Bill mentioned in his talk was his experience as an impressionable youngster in a public school," Dr. Caraman said. "I want you parents to think about that. I want you parents to read your children's textbooks, read them carefully! Watch for the sly ways that secular humanism *permeates* those textbooks! Internationalism, sex education, evolution, situational ethics! All these things disparage and belittle the concepts we've always held dear, all our fundamental moral values the Bible teaches us. Even many Christian schools sometimes fail to see the far-reaching effects of these books and teachings that have all but taken over the minds of our children . . ."

Roxie glanced at her mother. Marian's hands were still, folded loosely in her lap, her eyes were focused directly on the pulpit, her lips slightly parted.

"You are parents!" Dr. Caraman was shouting. "You are loving, caring guardians of the future of this great nation—its children! It's up to you! You don't have to be teachers yourselves, or have any kind of specialized fancy-named degrees in order to rise as an army and be an effective force in the educational system!"

They stood on the steps of the church, blinking their eyes against the bright sunlight.

"Wasn't Dr. Caraman fine today!" Cynthia Preger said.

"He's always fine," Joe said. "And by the way, how'd you like that other fella there, Bess, honey? You may not be so fond of baseball, but say, weren't you impressed with his testimony today? And how 'bout you, Roxie? You like baseball?"

"Yeah . . . I like it . . ."

"He's one heck of a second baseman, all right, isn't he, Frank?"

"Sure is, Joe. Sure is."

"There are the Hawleys," Cynthia said, waving. "Wanda? Lew? Hi, there!"

The Hawleys moved through the crowd on the steps toward them.

" 'Morning, folks," Lew Hawley said cheerfully. He was holding his wife's arm. "We were looking for Louise. You haven't seen her, have you?"

"I thought I saw her with Lee-Ann," Bess offered. "I think they were going to the ladies' room."

"Oh, well, then I guess we'll just chat here with you a minute and we'll catch her when she comes out," Wanda Hawley said and leaned against a column. "My, sure is warm, isn't it?"

"I love it," Marian said. "Back in Syracuse, we'd be

wearing sweaters in early fall. I feel as if I'm still enjoying summer."

"*I* know summer's over," Roxie said, "because I'm back at school!"

"How do you like it, Roxie?" Louise's mother asked.

"It's okay," Roxie said.

"Interesting what Clem Caraman said about the schools, wasn't it?" Cynthia Preger said.

"Oh, yes. Well, I don't worry about Louise," Wanda Hawley said. "I know S.H.C.A.'s got the right books and teachers. Lew does look over her academic work, though, don't you, Lew?"

But Lew, who had grabbed Thomas John Seeds' shoulder as he passed them, didn't hear her. He was shaking Seeds' hand as if he hadn't seen him in ages.

"How're y'all?" Seeds said with a nod to the others.

"Hi, Diane!" Roxie said, kneeling down to greet the little girl hanging onto her father's leg.

"Hi, Roxie!" Diane Seeds answered shyly. "H'lo, Bess."

"Hi, Bess," a blonde girl said, tossing her hair.

"You folks met my older girl, Molly?" Seeds said.

"These are the Cables, our new neighbors," Cynthia said to Seeds and Molly. "I guess li'l Diane knows Roxie from Camp Deliverance, don't you, honey?"

"I'm pleased to meet y'all," Molly said. "I hope you like Howerton."

Marian said, "Thank you, Molly. It's nice to meet you, too."

"Well, we better be gettin' home," Thomas John said, with another nod. "Come on, now, Diane, let go my leg, now let go, hear?"

"Bye, now," Molly said softly, as her father steered her and her sister toward their car.

"I'll see y'all tomorrow morning, Tommy-John," Lew Hawley called. "Here's our girl, Wanda . . . Over here, Louise!"

"Lew thinks the world of Tommy-John Seeds," Cynthia said to Marian after the Hawleys had gone home with Louise. "He's raising his young ones practically by himself, his wife, Eileen, being sick so much of the time. Diane, she's still little and his older boy, he's a hard worker, but that Molly, my goodness . . ."

"That sweet blonde girl?" Marian asked.

"That sweet blonde girl's the one I told you about, remember? The one who was banging on a young man's door at all hours of the night?"

"Oh . . . That was Molly Seeds?"

"It surely was! I heard she was pregnant, but I can't believe it because I know Tommy-John'd never let her— well, you know, get an abortion or anything like that! But, honestly, nothing that girl's done would surprise me."

"She seems so sweet, polite . . ."

"Yes, well, as I said, good Christian teachings and prayers have helped Molly see the light, I do believe."

VIII

Roxie dumped her armful of books on the floor, careless of the markers and papers that spilled out at her feet. *"Why?"* she demanded.

Marian was calm. She looked at the books on the floor and then into her daughter's face. "Because we just feel it's the right thing to do, your father and I."

"To pull me out of school? That's the right thing to do?"

"We're not pulling you out of school, honey, we're enrolling you in a school we feel will be so much better for you."

"What makes you think Stafford Hill is better for me than Marble Avenue?"

Marian licked her lips. "We feel," she said slowly, "that the kinds of things they're doing in some of the public schools and the kinds of people you'll be associating with all the time there—well, it just might not be the healthiest atmosphere for a young person."

Roxie stared at her mother.

"Roxie, don't look at me that way," Marian said. "I've

seen things. And heard things. I've never felt really secure about Marble Avenue . . . And besides, I thought
you'd be happy, being with Bess and Hope and the other
girls you liked so much this summer. You do like them,
don't you?"

Roxie felt her heart beating rapidly. She knelt to gather
her books together.

"Don't you like them?" Marian repeated.

"Yes, I like them," Roxie said, not looking at her. "I
just thought that you'd talk to me about something like
this, without just springing it on me!" And when Marian didn't answer, she said, "Well, I do have something
to say about it, don't I?"

"Like . . . what?" Marian asked.

"Like, I think Marble Avenue is okay and I'm beginning to make some nice friends there. And I like the
teachers. Is this Mrs. Preger's idea or something?"

"No, it's my idea. And your father's. As I said. I can't
help worrying, Roxie. And as Dr. Caraman pointed out,
we are your loving, caring guardians, after all. And I
really do believe that the schools are doing very little to
encourage strong moral values in a self-centered society."

"You sound just like him! Dr. Caraman! And Mrs.
Preger, too!" Roxie said. She got up from the floor.
"You don't sound like *you* anymore, Mom!"

"Oh, honey, of course I'm *me*," Marian said, moving
to hug her. Roxie turned away. "I haven't changed, I've
only discovered new things. No, old things, really, but
things I never thought much about before. Now I see
ways in which I can work for the good, traditional values we've always believed in. I didn't realize before that

little people can make a difference! And if we all stick together, we can begin to change the awful things we see happening in our country and even in the world! Don't you see, Roxie?"

"I don't see you as a great crusader," Roxie said. "And I don't see Marble Avenue as some kind of reform school, either. I think it's just plain silly, that's what I think. What is it, anyway, my sex education course? Or Mary Carol Briley? Or is it because my science teacher says we were once apes?"

"Stop it, Roxie . . ."

"Well, don't I have any say in this?"

Marian sighed. "Sit down, honey . . ."

"I don't want to sit down!"

"Please?" She went over to the sofa, but Roxie remained standing.

"I talked to Dr. Arman . . . He's the principal over at S.H.C.A.," Marian said. "And it wasn't easy getting you enrolled. They seemed to be well filled up in the tenth grade. But because of my work with the church and our joining, and because of the Pregers and others who have put in a good word for us—oh, and also because of your work this past summer at the camp—"

"—they took me in out of the goodness of their hearts, right?"

"They would welcome you to Stafford Hill."

"Isn't there an interview?" Roxie asked. "Don't they have to talk to me or something? Bess said they did when she was telling me about the school . . ."

"There won't be an interview. They know you're a good Christian girl . . ."

"Did you say I was saved?"

"No, not exactly. I think that kind of thing comes over a period of time and that it just happens through exposure and—"

"Then it's all done? That's it?"

Marian looked down at her lap.

"When do I go?"

"Well, you'll finish out this week at Marble and start at Stafford Hill on Monday."

"Monday!" Roxie cried. "I've only been going to Marble for five weeks! That's hardly anything! Monday? I have to start *Monday?*" Clutching her books, she ran up the stairs to her room.

"Well, I knew it was only a matter of time," Mary Carol sighed.

"You knew more than I did," Roxie grumbled. "It was a complete shock to me. I thought at least I'd finish out the term here and by that time, maybe they'd see it wasn't Sodom and Gomorrah—but I have to start Monday!"

"Really? That soon? You mean this is your last week?"

Roxie nodded glumly.

"Well, honey-babe, it's been awful nice knowing you. I wish you a lot of luck with your life," Mary Carol said, patting Roxie's shoulder.

"Oh, come on," Roxie said, "we'll see each other all the time."

"No, we won't, Roxie. Really. It's a whole 'nother life over there. We sinners don't mix much with the born-agains. We're lost, remember . . ."

"Knock it off," Roxie said.

"I'm not kidding you," Mary Carol said. "Some of the S.H. kids are so wild when they're on their own we just can't believe it. And some of 'em are falling on their knees every minute praying, and we just can't hardly handle that either! But I'll be thinking about you, Roxie, and really hoping that it all works out for you. You're a real nice person. Try not to let 'em change you."

That night after dinner, Bess Preger came to see Roxie.

"She's in her room," Marian told Bess. "I think she's upset with us."

"She'll be all right, Mrs. Cable. She's probably nervous about starting at a new place again, but she already knows a lot of kids and she's going to be real happy. You'll see."

"I hope so, Bess. Go right on up and knock. Oh, and Bess?"

"Yes, ma'am?"

"Thank you so much for coming over. That was very thoughtful."

Bess knocked. When there was no response, she knocked again.

"Roxie?" she called softly. "Roxie? It's Bess. Can I come in?" She heard Roxie's gruff, "Sure," and opened the door.

"Hi . . ."

"Hello," Roxie said.

Bess wasted no time. She rushed to Roxie, who was sitting on her bed with her knees under her chin, and hugged her, knees and all.

"Roxie, I am just so glad you're going to be with us. I have prayed so hard for it, I honestly have. Roxie, you're not going to be sorry for one single minute. The people and the teachers are just the loveliest you could meet anywhere and they'll be so happy to welcome you."

Roxie looked at her.

"I mean it. You are going to feel so wanted, why you just won't believe it! I promise you, Roxie. And I'm going to make it my personal responsibility to see that you never feel alone at Stafford Hill."

Roxie let herself smile for the first time. Then she let out a little sigh. "That's really nice of you, Bess," she said. She wondered if she'd have done the same thing for someone that Bess was doing for her.

"It's my pleasure, Roxie," Bess said, returning Roxie's smile.

Roxie was indeed called Roseanne by her teachers, as Hope had once predicted. That, after all, was the name on her registration card and she didn't bother to ask them to use her nickname. She hardly said anything. She watched a lot.

"They talk about accepting things with joy," she told her father. "Even bad things. They say it makes you stronger. 'We glory in tribulations also: knowing that tribulation worketh patience; And patience, experience; and experience, hope,' " she quoted.

Francis smiled. "Quoting the Bible, eh?"

"We have to memorize. For class. That was Romans. Chapter five. Verses three and four."

"Well," Francis said, grinning. "*I'm* impressed . . . But tell me; what's so bad about being able to accept even bad things with joy?"

"Nothing, Daddy, but I don't think *I* can do it."

"Don't worry about it, Roxie," Lee-Ann said.

"I'm not worried. It's only that I'm not really like you, Lee-Ann. I *like* rock 'n' roll. And boys. And clothes and gossip and fun! I don't see what's so wrong about that."

"Oh, Roxie, we like boys and clothes and we like to have fun, too!" Lee-Ann answered. "What we mean by separating is that there's fun and *fun*, know what I mean? You have to know what's important and valuable. You have to know when you're being tempted and tested by the Devil. The gods people worship in this world are destroying us!"

Dear Glenna,

They changed my school. I'm out of Marble Avenue now and in Stafford Hill. I was really so mad when Mom told me I was being changed because nobody even asked me if I wanted to go. It's not that Stafford Hill is terrible or anything, it's just that I wasn't even consulted about it. Bess Preger and some other girls I met go there and they're very friendly and nice, but I was starting to make friends at Marble, too, like Mary Carol Briley, who took me to a party a couple of weeks ago. In fact, I bet that party had something to do with their decision because Daddy saw some kids making out and I mentioned there was grass there, though

I didn't even take any. He didn't push it or anything, but I bet!

Mom and Dad are really getting on the world's case now. I mean about how we're all losing our traditional values and turning to drugs and pornography and all that. I guess it's really Mom, but Dad kind of goes along. And Stafford Hill says we all need to turn back to God before it's too late and we're all destroyed. Most of that goes right over my head, but meanwhile, here I am starting all over again having to meet new kids and new teachers just when I thought I was beginning to get settled.

I can't wait until Thanksgiving. Can't you make it come faster?

Love,
Roxie

Dear Rox,

The same day your letter arrived I got a glowing one from Mom all about your new school. She makes it sound like a combination cure-for-all-diseases and an educational heaven. I don't know much about the school, but I have seen ol' Clem Caraman on the tube—not his early-Sunday-morning program, thank you, but on the news occasionally. Certainly does his best to influence legislation, doesn't he? But I really can't see Mom and Dad falling too far into that, or all that evangelical stuff, either, for that matter. And if you like the kids, Mom seems to feel that the curriculum is terrific.

Listen, Rox, maybe it's a good change for you—small private school and all that. Your main complaint seems to be that everyone acted without any say-so on your part, and while I'm not wild for that, it might turn out well. In fact, it probably will because I know you. You always make your own happiness wherever you are. So don't worry. Just don't start thumping the Bible at me or I'll thump right back!

My crazy roommate, Caroline, is dating a vice president at my office. Can you imagine? I've given her a list of working-condition improvements I'd like her to present to him at their next cozy dinner.

Sorry, honey, I can't make Thanksgiving come any quicker. Maybe your Dr. Caraman can, with his connections!

Love,
Glen

Roxie was assigned more homework than she'd ever had before. Math was still her weakest subject, but her father helped her with it. She found she liked citizenship and grammar-and-composition and home economics. She tolerated weekly chapel and religious study courses.

"Mrs. Bates says that before salvation, man is an enemy of God. I never thought of myself as an enemy of God," she told her parents.

"You're not. It's just a way of putting things," Francis said.

"No, they mean it," Roxie insisted. "That's supposed to be your condition if you haven't been born again. If you're not saved before Armageddon comes you'll perish in the Tribulations. When Christ comes again He'll preserve only the ones who are saved." She looked directly at her mother. "Are you saved, Mom?"

"Well . . . I . . ." Marian took a breath. "I—accept Jesus as my personal savior . . ." she said.

"You don't sound absolutely sure, like Mrs. Preger," Roxie said.

"Well, I'm not as adamant as Mrs. Preger . . . exactly," Marian said hesitantly. "But I do believe in all the basic things the church stands for . . . and I do accept Jesus . . . I'm just waiting . . . to find out how I'm supposed to serve, what's expected of me. Dr. Lloyd—in my Bible class?—he says that a new convert must 'wait patiently before the Lord to be taught of Him.' He says that a Christian has no right to take more than one step at a time, and that to make a plan is always a mistake. The Holy Spirit in your life will make all the plans and your life will be unveiled on a moment by moment basis. So, I guess I'm just . . . taking it . . . one step at a time. I like everything behind it, Roxie."

Roxie snorted. "What about you, Daddy?" she asked. "Are you saved?"

Francis caught his wife's eye before answering.

"Look Rox," he said finally, "I work hard at my job. I consider myself a good Christian and I believe in a lot of what they stand for over at Stafford Hill. Okay. Dr. Caraman gets a little extreme for me at times, but I can't say I'm overly bothered by it . . . I just figure I'll take the good parts and leave the rest and get through life trying to do the best I can . . . That's all . . ."

Roxie frowned. "I don't think you're supposed to leave out the parts you don't like," she said. She thought a moment. "What about Glenna?" she asked.

"What about her?"

"Have you written to her about Stafford Hill?"

"I have," Marian said, "but she never says a thing about it in her replies."

"I wrote her about changing schools," Roxie said. "But

she just said I could make myself happy anywhere if I try. I wish she'd come home. I can't wait for Thanksgiving . . ."

Roxie called Mary Carol Briley but felt anxious each time. She wasn't sure if a tiny change in Mary Carol's voice or attitude was real or imagined.

"How're y'all doin'?" Mary Carol asked. Was it friendliness, Roxie wondered, or wariness.

But she answered, "Oh, fine! How're you? How's Bobbie? How's Emily? Can we get together?"

They did, once or twice, but Roxie felt somehow isolated, and unsure whose fault it was.

She slept badly, waking every few hours and tossing around in her bed, turning her pillow, pulling on and kicking off her blankets.

One Saturday morning, awake before her parents, she made herself a cup of herb tea and went into the living room. She sat with her tea on her father's footstool, facing the gray blankness of the television screen.

Roxie giggled in spite of herself. When her friends had slept over on a Friday night back in Syracuse, they usually turned on the set in Glenna's large room and laughed at the Saturday-morning cartoons. Then they either fell asleep again or stayed up and continued their conversation of the night before.

She wished Marge were there now. She flicked on the TV in a nostalgic mood, all ready to either laugh or cry.

"—remember, my friends, it is a toll-free call. The number is there at the bottom of your screen. We are waiting for your call, waiting to send you this brochure with all the facts about our brand new retirement home—"

Dr. Caraman, Roxie thought. There he is, close up. This is what you get down here instead of Tom and Jerry.

But she didn't switch him off or turn the channel. She stared at him: the thickness of his salt-and-pepper hair, the fierce slant of his eyebrows. He looks so much taller on television, Roxie thought.

"—and as soon as we receive your call, we'll send you the brochure along with this 'power of God' bumper sticker—"

Roxie sighed.

"—and we were speaking, my friends, about promises and responsibilities. Promises—and—responsibilities! Acknowledge your responsibilities and the God of Peace shall reward you. Let us look together at Psalm 34, David: 'I sought the Lord and He heard me, and delivered me from all my fears.' You must seek the Lord, you must *seek* Him, 'I will bless the Lord at all times: His praise shall continually be in my mouth.' You must *seek* the Lord to be received of His blessings, for unless you—"

Roxie clicked off the set.

The very next Monday after school, Bess approached Roxie at her locker.

"Where're you going, Miss Cable?" Bess asked cheerfully.

"Home . . ." Roxie said with a shrug.

"That's what I thought," Bess said. "I know it seems as if I've been neglectful of you, but I've really had my eye on you all along. Oh, Roxie, I just kept hoping you'd jump right into things all by yourself with your new insights and all, but I guess you still need a big sister for a while now, don't you?"

"Oh, Bess—" Roxie protested, but Bess just smiled.

"No, now enough of this moping around, you're coming with me. There's a new ministry being formed of high school kids to work with mentally retarded kids our age. Now you know you'd be wonderful with them, Roxie, and instead of sitting at home alone you should be busy in service to the Lord. You just see if that doesn't make you feel useful and wanted and so much better!"

She went at first because of Bess's coaxing, but gradually she became involved in the work. She loved the children. And there were often church-related socials, roller-skating parties and picnics at which she saw some of the boys in her classes. Only one, Harold Pointer, paid any attention to her. But she thought Harold was just a big tease and wore his hair too short besides.

The time passed quickly and that's what Roxie wanted.

"Roseanne?"

"Yes, Miss Gordon?"

Roxie's English teacher held out a large manilla envelope stuffed with leaflets. "These are for the Prime of Life Ministry meeting on Saturday. Will you take them over to the prayer chapel, please? Dr. Arman's waiting for them."

"Yes, ma'am," Roxie answered as she rose and took the envelope. The Prime of Life Ministry was composed of senior citizens, members of Stafford Hill, who volunteered for special services and were sent on visitations to the sick and infirm and formed evangelical teams to send to rest homes, churches and other meeting places. Roxie was constantly amazed at the number of ministries and volunteers who served them. There were many jobs for teens, too, and Roxie was toying with the idea of joining a visiting singing ministry.

Strolling behind the school, daydreaming and humming to herself, she was all the more startled when a rhododendron bush rustled its leaves at her. She drew in her breath and stopped short.

The rhododendron bush gave a low chuckle. Suddenly, a laughing-faced boy leaped up out of the bush and cried, "Scared ya, huh!"

Roxie drew in her breath and nodded.

The boy stepped out from behind the bush. "It's a good place to smoke," he explained. "If they see the smoke coming from the bush they think the building's on fire and by the time they come back with the entire state's volunteer fire departments and the F.B.I., I'm sitting at my desk reading Isaiah!" He grinned and Roxie laughed. "Want a drag?" he asked, holding out a cigarette stub.

"No . . ." Roxie said, shaking her head.

He ground the cigarette out with his shoe. "I know you," he said. "Roseanne—uh—Cable. Right? Louise Hawley's friend?"

Roxie nodded, staring at the boy's friendly tanned face and curly brown hair.

"You know who I am?"

"Jarrell Meek," Roxie said.

He leaned toward her and whispered, "What did Louise tell you about me? Because it's all lies!"

"Nothing," Roxie said, smiling.

"*That's* a lie," Jarrell said.

Roxie laughed. "She said you were a member of the Mafia and you were sent to Howerton to organize the garbage collectors!"

Jarrell laughed out loud. He had a warm, deep laugh. He liked to carve whistles out of wood, he played a mean game of poker, he liked to shock and startle and most of all he liked to laugh.

"You're from up north?" he asked.

"Yes . . . Upstate New York."

"New York," Jarrell said. "I'll get there someday. Maybe tomorrow."

"I have to go," Roxie said, glancing down at the envelope tucked under her arm. "I'm late."

"I'll walk you. Where're you going?"

"The prayer chapel . . ."

"Dr. Caraman's in there," Jarrell said. "But I'll risk it to walk you over."

"Thanks a lot," Roxie said. "What'll he do when he sees you?"

Jarrell straightened his back, tucked his chin into his neck and spoke in a deep, clear voice. "He'll say, 'Are you pleasing God today, Jarrell?' and I'll say, 'Yes, sir,' and he'll say, 'A wise son maketh a glad father: but a foolish son is the heaviness of his mother.' "

"And what will you say?"

"I'll say, 'My father's glad, sir,' and he'll laugh and muss up my hair."

They found Dr. Arman, the principal, and Dr. Caraman in conversation when they arrived at the prayer chapel. Roxie was nervous—she'd never seen Clement Caraman this close. Against her will, she'd been impressed that her mother had talked with an international celebrity, someone who was seen and heard by millions of people. "Ah, Jarrell Meek!" Dr. Caraman said. "Are you giving God pleasure today?"

Roxie gaped.

"Yes, sir," Jarrell answered and grinned.

"Then why aren't you in class, studying His word?"

"I'm accompanying the new girl, sir. To show her where things are," Jarrell answered.

"Mmmmm," Dr. Caraman said skeptically. "Is your father glad today, Jarrell?"

"He's very glad, sir," Jarrell answered.

Smiling, Dr. Caraman turned to Roxie. "Miss Roseanne Cable," he said, with a small nod of his head.

"Yes, sir," Roxie said, respectfully. She was again impressed.

"Welcome to Howerton and to the Stafford Hill Christian Academy. I've had the pleasure of chatting with your lovely mother. We are indeed grateful for your family's prayerful support." He nodded again and exited quickly. Roxie was staring after him when Dr. Arman coughed.

"Oh—excuse me, Dr. Arman—" She held out the envelope of leaflets. "These—uh—Mrs. Bates said these were for the Prime of Life—?"

"It's all right, Roseanne," the principal said with a smile. "He has that effect on everybody."

Jarrell laughed loudly.

Roxie found Jarrell waiting for her after school. She gave him an embarrassed smile and headed resolutely for the school bus, but he stopped her with a wave.

"How far do you live?" he asked.

"A mile . . . about."

"Why don't you walk today?" He cocked his head. "I'll walk you."

His southern accent was not as pronounced as Bess's or some of the others'. She wondered if he'd always lived in the South but decided not to ask him.

"Well . . ." she said, "I'd better take the bus."

"Come on," he urged. "It's a beautiful day."

Roxie glanced up. Everyone on the bus was looking at her from the windows.

"Maybe another time," she murmured and hurried down the path, remembering what the girls had said about Jarrell Meek.

She looked back once and found him staring at her.

"He's wild," Bess said that evening as she and Roxie studied together.

"How do you mean, wild?" Roxie asked.

"He borrows cars from his friends at Marble and they cruise the streets at night. He drinks . . . He hangs out at roadhouses . . . And he seduces girls!"

"Oh, Bess! He's only a junior in high school!"

"Well, Lisa Evans kind of hinted he was the one who made her sister pregnant."

"Do you believe that?" Roxie asked.

Bess shrugged. "I don't know," she said, "but I do know that he likes to break rules. He's real charming, I guess you saw that for yourself, and Louise has had a crush on him since fourth grade. I guess I like him, too, but he's wild, Roxie. Someday he won't be able to use his charm to get out of stuff and he'll be expelled. You'll see—'He that perverteth his ways shall be known.' "

IX

"I visited the White House, yes, the White House, the stately home of our President and the Presidents before him, the symbol of American democracy, and at dinner I sat at the President's table, the President's table, and do you know how I felt? Do you know how I felt? I felt honored. Honored and privileged as the President made known to me his loving and prayerful support of our church and our ministries and our work to bring God back into the hearts of our people and give us all a purpose for living once more!"

Roxie looked from Dr. Caraman's face above the pulpit to his televised face on the cameraman's screen next to her in the aisle. The picture was black-and-white, and she thought how much more impressive he looked in living color, with his dark blue suit and red-and-blue tie against the white and pale green walls behind him. His face flushed each time he brought his hand down hard against the sides of the pulpit as he repeated his phrases for emphasis. She found herself hoping that the camera up front, facing the congregation, would choose her for a close-up so that she could call Glenna and perhaps her friends Marge and Peter and Ellie, and tell them to watch when this particular taped service would be aired in Syracuse. Dr. Caraman had said that Stafford Hill had close to three hundred television and radio networks across the country, and that its dream was to someday broadcast overseas. She tried to put an attentive and rapt expression on her face.

"—and we need *your* loving and prayerful support, too," Dr. Caraman went on. "Call the toll-free number you see on your screen right now and give us your pledge to help our ministries! When you do, you will receive *two* prepublication fifth-revision copies of the King James version of the Bible, put together by scholars from many revered Christian institutions." Dr. Caraman held up one of the copies and smiled at it. "It's the latest revision, it is bound in fine, simulated leather, and you will receive *two:* one for Mom, one for Dad, something you will each treasure always, and what we ask is that you call now and make your pledge in loving support of our work. Our people are waiting to tell the Bates-Baxter Publishing House to print up *your* very own copies right now and get them in the mail to you. The number is on your screen, it is toll-free—"

Roxie felt a hand on her arm and looked up at her mother, who smiled back at her and gave her wrist a little squeeze. Roxie leaned forward for a glimpse of her father two seats away. Francis's eyes were focused on the pulpit and he looked relaxed leaning against the backrest of the pew.

Across the aisle, Roxie recognized Jarrell's profile. She suddenly heard the tiny beeps of his digital watch alarm and she clapped her hand over her mouth to stifle a giggle. An older man next to Jarrell elbowed the boy's arm and Roxie frowned, wondering if the man were Jarrell's father or grandfather. She leaned forward. The woman on Jarrell's other side who brusquely patted Jarrell's knee was older, too, with iron-gray hair poking out from a navy blue hat. Roxie was still frowning when the booming voice of the guest preacher forced her attention away from the Meek family.

Jarrell Meek was sixteen. He thought a lot about being sixteen and how sometimes he felt like a man, older even than his own father, who was close to sixty. And he thought about the other times when he wanted to bawl like a two-year-old, or make a knot out of Louise Hawley's long brown hair. He wondered if he'd always have feelings like that, even when he was grown and on his own in the world. Having to sit still for long periods of time made all his bones itch and his head go as fuzzy as the TV reception in Howerton. Church and school were two places requiring long stretches of sitting still. He had trouble even listening to the guest, a country-western singer, newly come to Christ. When Dr. Caraman returned to the pulpit to condemn the Soviet Union for its persecution of Christians and Jews—"Send your letters to the Russian Premier, Moscow, U.S.S.R.!"—Jarrell began to fool with his watch again. He selected another time at random and hoped his alarm would beep at a moment of silence.

He felt a hand on his wrist. His father glared down at him. Jarrell pressed the stop-alarm button. Since his father had caught him in the act, he'd probably take the watch away from him.

"—Your letters should be courteous and prayerful—"

Jarrell slowly turned his head from side to side, looking for his friend, Kenny St. Pierre, and his family. If he found Kenny, maybe they could go somewhere together after church, away from their families. Maybe Kenny's brother would take them somewhere in his car . . .

He couldn't find Kenny, but he spotted Roxie. He winked at her and smiled.

His father was opening his hymn book. Jarrell had missed the announcement of the hymn, but suddenly everyone was singing "Washed in the Blood of the Lamb," and he knew the first two verses of that one by heart. He sang loudly and smiled up at his father. Singing was something Jarrell did very well and he often showed off his voice in church and at prayer meetings. Dr. Caraman had told him that he might someday be invited to join the Christian Grace College Choir, like Patty Preger, and travel all over the world.

Jarrell wanted to sing all over the world, but not hymns and certainly not with the Christian Grace College Choir. He wasn't going to college at all—he was going to play electric guitar and join a rock group and get out of Howerton just as soon as he was able. His friend Bill Wooster, who was a senior at Marble Avenue, was teaching him how to play. Nobody knew that, not even Kenny. And as soon as he felt ready to turn professional, he'd be gone.

The service was winding down. Jarrell yawned. He

decided that if he couldn't find Kenny in the crowd on the way out, at least he knew where Roxie was . . .

The Cables paused in the entranceway of the church. They were waiting to go home with the Pregers, but the Pregers had to find Patty, who had been brought by bus from the college to sing in the choir. Francis was thinking that though the car would be crowded, it was easier to park one car than two on a Sunday morning. He suddenly turned at the sound of a deep voice behind him.

"Good afternoon, Roxie. Are these your parents?"

Roxie turned and blushed furiously. "Yes . . ." she managed, and thought: The girls were right—he's such a con artist! She wanted to laugh.

"Aren't you going to introduce us?" Francis asked with a smile.

"This is Jarrell Meek," Roxie mumbled as Jarrell held out his hand for Francis to shake. She tried to catch his eye but he wouldn't look at her.

"I'm pleased to meet you, sir," Jarrell said, and nodded at Marian. "Ma'am . . ."

"We're pleased to meet you, Jarrell," Marian said. "Are you in Roxie's class at school?"

"He's a junior," Roxie said, and tried to kick him with the side of her foot.

"I saw you inside . . ." Jarrell said to Roxie, "and I was wondering if you'd like to go over to Arby's and have lunch? We could walk there from here and then maybe your father could pick you up. If he's not busy or anything."

Francis opened his mouth to assure Jarrell he wasn't busy but Roxie spoke first.

"Thank you, but I can't. We're having lunch with Bess's family."

"Oh," Jarrell said. "Well . . ."

Another boy approached. "Hi," he said, with a nod to Roxie and then, more enthusiastically, "Hi, Jar!"

"Oh, hi, Kenny," Jarrell said. "Maybe another time, okay, Roxie? Nice to have met you folks!" He moved swiftly out of the crowd with his friend.

"We're not having lunch with the Pregers today," Francis said. "He seemed like a nice boy. Why didn't you want to go with him?"

"I just didn't feel like it," Roxie said, looking away. "Besides, Louise likes him and I don't want to butt in."

"He didn't ask Louise, he asked you," Marian said with a smile. "Does he drive a car?"

"I don't know," Roxie answered. "Why?"

"Well, you know you can't go in a car unchaperoned."

"Well, but he didn't *say*—"

"I know," Marian interrupted. "That's what I meant. He seems to be a nice, considerate boy. It he does drive, he didn't suggest taking you off by yourself."

Oh, no, he wouldn't suggest that to anyone's parents, Roxie thought. Whatever Jarrell Meek was, he was certainly different from any other boy she'd met. Even Peter . . .

Bess had told Roxie that S.H.C.A. students and church members were not allowed to travel in cars without an adult present, even on a double date. There had been no rule like that in Syracuse. Glenna had dated all through high school and her parents hadn't stopped her.

Roxie was silent in the car driving home. Near a shopping center, they passed a girl who looked like Mary Carol and she spun around quickly in the seat, but the girl's face was turned away.

Roxie decided to join Youthlight, a church club for teen-agers which taught them basic missionary work. Some of its members went soul-winning door-to-door, but Roxie was interested in activities such as singing before school assemblies, visiting bedridden and hospitalized youngsters and doing crafts work: making puppets and stuffed pillows and religious posters. She was not as surprised as Mrs. Curran, Youthlight's advisor, when Jarrell Meek joined, too. But she decided to tease him by asking his reason.

"I like to sing," he said with a shrug. "I sing real well. Haven't you ever heard me sing? Listen."

"Not now!" Roxie said and giggled. "Everybody's making puppets now! Did you know we're doing a show at Mason General tonight after supper?"

"Of course I know," Jarrell told her. "I'm singing 'There Is Joy in that Land.' Solo!"

"Solo?"

"You bet. Just for you. To impress you. You haven't been too impressed with me so far."

That wasn't entirely true. Roxie's days were more exciting since she became aware that Jarrell was watching her. Each walk down a hall to class, each bite of a sandwich in the cafeteria, each facial expression during a church service, Roxie tried to carry off with a casual but definite flair.

"You're right," she said. "You're not too impressive."

"I'm trying. Listen," he said seriously. "Your friends went home after school today. You don't know anyone that well on the activities bus who's going to be watching you with Stafford Hill's most notorious character. Let me walk you home. I'll be impressive, I swear."

"Don't swear," Roxie said laughing, and Jarrell said, "Sh-oot!"

Roxie considered. "Well, but if I walk home," she said, "I'll be really late and I might not get all my work done before supper and then I'll have to go out to the hospital for the show right after that. I can't, Jarrell. I'd better take the bus."

"Finish your work when you get home tonight. It won't be late, they're only little kids in that ward. They'll have to go to bed early . . . Aw, come on, Roxie, don't be like those other simps you hang out with! Let your hair down, I won't bite you for Chr- for Pete's sake!"

His efforts to impress her made her laugh. On the way home he played upon the idea that she'd been ashamed to be seen with him; he maneuvered her close to buildings, kept his head down, moved his eyes back and forth furtively. If someone walked toward them, he pushed her quickly behind a tree, peering out only when he was sure the person had passed. He ducked behind litter baskets along the curbs, letting her walk on by herself, even if she were in midsentence. When they finally reached a back residential street and Roxie was still laughing but exasperated, he stopped his clowning and tenderly took her hand.

Roxie prayed fervently her hand wouldn't sweat. The sudden, out-of-the-blue way he'd reached for her thrilled her more than anything she could remember. She was ice cold and hot. She wondered briefly if this was how you were supposed to feel when you got saved.

At first, Jarrell seemed as content as Roxie to keep their meetings secret. Nothing was said, but he approached her only after club meetings or when they were both sure no one else was around. He made no effort to walk with her when Bess was waiting or when everyone had piled on the bus and was looking out the windows.

Finally, he asked if he could come over one Friday night. She thought about it. She wondered what Bess would think or say if she saw him arriving. And worse, she didn't know what she would do if Bess were to drop over while he was there.

She expressed none of these fears to Jarrell. And she knew that even if any of those things were to happen, it was a chance she was willing to take.

Her mother and father were delighted that Roxie was going to entertain "that nice young man" they'd met at church. Marian baked her special chocolate cake that Glenna and her friends had always begged for.

He was due to arrive at seven-thirty. Long before that,

Roxie had done her hair three different ways. When Jarrell hadn't shown up by ten of eight, she was almost in tears.

The doorbell rang at eight. Roxie's heart was beating so loudly, she had to rush into the bathroom to wash her face and calm herself down.

Francis was the one who greeted a panting Jarrell.

"I'm really sorry I'm late," he breathed. "I had to run an unexpected errand for a friend."

"That's all right," Francis said and shook Jarrell's hand. "Rox!"

Roxie appeared, looking nonchalant.

"Hi, Jarrell," she said, crossed the room and flopped onto the couch.

"Hi. Sorry I'm late," he repeated in case she hadn't heard. "I ran the whole way." He was wearing a light blue shirt, chinos and a lightweight jacket.

"I'll—uh—see if your mother needs anything," Francis said and beat a retreat to the kitchen.

Jarrell sat down next to Roxie.

"Hi," he said again.

She didn't look at him. "Hi," she murmured.

"Are you mad that I'm late?"

"No . . ."

"I had to help Kenny."

"Oh."

"Have you got—" he began as she said, "Do you want—" and they both laughed, embarrassed.

"What were you going to say?" Roxie asked.

"No, you."

"I was just going to ask you if you wanted a cold drink or something," she said.

"Um, yeah, that's what I was going to ask you for. My throat's a little dry . . ."

Glad for something to do, she ran to get it. While she was gone, Jarrell took several deep breaths and leaned back on the couch.

When she returned, he tensed up again and sat forward. Their fingers touched as she handed him the glass and both were very aware of it.

He sipped his drink slowly and didn't speak until it was almost drained.

Finally, he said, "Roxie?"

"Mmm?"

"Listen, I know you can't go out with me in a car . . . Right?"

She shrugged slightly. "I guess . . ." she said.

His eyes widened. "Would you?" he asked.

She looked at him without speaking.

"Did your church let you go out? Without a chaperone, I mean? I mean, the church where you came from."

"Oh, yes . . . We could go out with boys who drove . . . That's if our parents knew the boy and everything . . ."

Jarrell wiped his eyebrow with his thumb. "Y'know, sometimes . . . the things you're not supposed to want . . . Well, I want them. You know what I mean?"

She nodded.

"Do you like rock 'n' roll?"

"Yeah . . ."

"Do you listen to it?" he asked.

"You know, to tell you the truth, I haven't had time," she said. "Between homework and school and clubs . . .

I hardly ever put on my records or watch TV any more."

"That's what they try for," Jarrell muttered. "To keep you so busy with the Bible you don't want to do anything they think is sinful. Like just listening to rock 'n' roll, for Pete's sake . . ."

Roxie glanced up to see if her parents were within earshot. She couldn't tell.

"Well," she said, finally, "I'm busy, all right . . ."

"I don't want to be busy that way all the time," he said. "It's not enough for me. Besides . . ."

"Besides what?"

"Are your parents strict with you?"

"I don't think so . . . Not really . . ."

"Mine are." Jarrell got up from the couch and began to pace. "They try to be. They were when I was younger. And they still are when they get mad enough. Especially my father. My mother . . . She's . . . she's pretty frail now . . ." He stretched his arms and cracked his knuckles. "See, they thought they'd had all their kids by the time I came along." He barked a laugh. "I was a big surprise. My brother and two sisters are long gone . . . married . . ."

Roxie wondered if this was why he'd asked to see her, to say these things, to talk about himself, or if it were spontaneous. She wasn't sure how to respond and she wanted to be sure to say the right thing.

"Do you believe—" she began, "what they believe? I mean, are you religious in their way?"

"I believe in God," Jarrell said firmly, "but I don't believe He disapproves if I play music or go to movies or—or anything like that. And I sure don't believe He wants the St. Pierres to go without dinner so Clement Caraman can spend their paycheck!"

Roxie blinked. "What?" she asked.

Jarrell sat down again heavily. "That's why I was late tonight; I went out and bought a bucket of chicken for the St. Pierres because Kenny's father turned his paycheck over to the church. They didn't even have enough for dinner!"

"But—but . . . Did Dr. Caraman *ask* them to do that?" Roxie stammered, shocked.

"Nah, not in so many words. But he sure makes it plain he expects everyone's 'support,' and there's an awful lot of guilty feelings if you don't come up with your 'share.' Listen, the St. Pierres aren't the only ones who give their lives over to Stafford Hill. You'd be surprised. You'd be surprised who goes without food and warm coats . . ."

Roxie's frown deepened. "But, *why?*" she asked, as her mother appeared in the doorway with a tray.

"I thought you two could use a snack," she said.

Jarrell looked up and smiled. "Thank you, ma'am," he said, "we sure could."

When Marian left, Roxie said, "But how can Kenny go to S.H.C.A.? It's expensive, it's a private school!"

"I know. I don't know where his father got the money. The guy works in a printing shop for coolie wages, and he won't let Kenny's mom work. You know . . . The woman's place is in the home and all that. He's real proud. They're strict with Kenny like my folks are with me. Or they try to be." He turned to her. "What I'm asking you, Roxie, is—well, you just joined Stafford Hill.

It was different where you came from. Maybe you're . . ."

"Maybe I'm what?" Suddenly she wondered what he wanted from her. "Maybe I'm like those girls you pick up when you go out in the car with your friends from Marble Avenue? Is that what you were going to ask me?"

He winced and kneaded his thigh with his fingers.

"No. I didn't mean that. What I meant was . . . See, there are two kinds of kids at the academy. There are the kids like Louise and"—he cocked his head toward the door—"Bess Preger, who get cardiac arrest if you so much as say 'damnation!' And then there are kids like Tom Kunkle and Steve Kreske and Molly Seeds and . . . and a whole bunch of kids who do stuff I wouldn't even tell you the minute they get out of school or their houses . . ."

"And you, too?" Roxie asked.

He looked down. "I'm not as bad as that," he said quietly. "I'm not as bad as you hear I am. I just don't go along with everything, is all . . ."

"Well," Roxie said, leaning a little toward him. "What was it you were going to ask me?"

He sighed. "The thing is, I just couldn't put you in either category. You know, wild or pious. I thought maybe . . . we could . . . go out together. And talk and things. Because I liked you right from the beginning. But I just don't get any 'peace' out of being saved the way they want." He looked at her. "Do you? I mean, *do* you?"

"I'm not sure I'm . . . exactly saved," she said tentatively. She was busily wondering if she *were* in a category. Pious like Bess and Louise or wild, like Molly

Seeds or . . . Jarrell? She was neither one. Wasn't it all right to be neither one?

He was grinning at her. "You're not saved?" he asked almost gleefully.

Roxie drew back. She wasn't sure what he was thinking. "Well," she said finally, "maybe you're supposed to work at it harder. Maybe the peace comes. That's what my mother says, anyhow. You're supposed to have a lot of discipline. Not focus on—"

"I know, not focus on the sins of the world. But I don't think reading books they don't approve of is a sin or watching TV or going to movies or drinking beer or going out with a girl without her big brother in the back seat . . . Listen, Roxie, I've been at this longer than you, and I did all the things I was taught, I witnessed, went to church, read the Bible, prayed . . ." He looked at her. "I get real restless, Roxie . . ."

Roxie worried about what her girlfriends would think if they knew she was spending time with Jarrell, though there was something exciting about the secrecy of it. Friendship and acceptance by the girls was important, so Roxie avoided an open relationship with Jarrell, telling herself there was no point in antagonizing her friends.

She had one bad moment. On an afternoon when a Youthlight meeting was cancelled, Hope arranged a baking party so that all the girls could make special treats for the opening of the Stafford Hill retirement home. But Roxie had earlier made plans with Jarrell for that suddenly empty afternoon.

"Roxie, the meeting's cancelled. Why, what else could you have planned?" Hope asked.

Roxie hated to lie. If she were seen with Jarrell, the other girls would know she had chosen to be with him instead of working with them.

She stood facing Hope, Bess, Lee-Ann and Louise, feeling terribly torn, wishing now that the Youthlight meeting had gone on as scheduled. She couldn't go with the girls and tell Jarrell she had chosen them, either . . .

"I can't," she said, squinting her eyes at Hope. "I just can't . . . I have this terrible headache—it started in gym and just got worse . . ." She pressed her fingers to her temples, sure that now she really did have a headache.

She gave the same excuse to Jarrell, and all of them sent her home after school with pats and sympathy. And Roxie did go right to bed with the shades in her room pulled down.

But except for that time, she was convinced she had it all. Her days were full. Life was beginning to be exciting.

And at last, Glenna came home for Thanksgiving.

X

"It's so good to see you all!" Glenna cried, hugging first one, then the other, then starting over again. "The house looks terrific! *You* look terrific! Oh, I missed you all so much . . ."

Roxie knew she'd missed her sister, but she didn't realize how deeply until she saw her. She kept staring at Glenna to make sure she was real. She certainly looked beautiful. Her black hair was parted in the middle and pulled up in the back over her ears, a new style for her. And she was wearing a lovely red wool suit that Roxie had never seen before. Her face glowed!

"Tell us about your job! Tell us about your apartment! Tell us about Caroline!" Roxie cried, bouncing up and down.

"I've told you!" Glenna laughed. "I've written you everything! Oh, Caroline's thinking of getting married!"

"Married! To that vice president at Burke-Masters?" Marian asked.

"No! Not him! This is somebody she met two weeks ago."

"Two weeks?"

"Caroline's like that!" Glenna laughed again. "She'll be with someone else two weeks from now. Tell me about *you!* Roxie. You're in the church choir?"

"No, not the one on television. Have you seen it? Do you watch the Sunday service?" she asked eagerly.

"Now, you know me," Glenna joked as they sat down at the table. "I don't stir on Sunday before noon!"

"Glenna," her mother said with a slight frown. "You haven't joined a church in New York?"

"Marian," Francis interrupted before Glenna could answer. "The girl just got home. Now . . . save her after dinner, not before, okay?"

"Frank, you're terrible!" Marian said.

They went upstairs after dinner to Roxie's room, where Glenna grew serious immediately.

"You're not really into that born-again Christian stuff are you, Rox?" she asked, looking into her sister's eyes. "I mean, just how committed are you to this?"

"I'm not into it like Mom is," Roxie said. "Or my friends. But I like them, Glen. They're really nice. They care about you . . ."

"Well, that part's okay," Glenna said. "But what about the rest of it? Do they give you all that stuff about burning in hell forever if you don't walk around with the Bible glued to your nose?"

Roxie laughed. "I'm really glad you're home, Glen," she said. "It's so good to talk to you!"

"Well, talk then," Glenna said. "You're making me nervous."

Roxie rested her chin in the palm of her hand and thought for a moment.

"The thing about being saved," she began, "is that when the great Tribulation comes, the ones who are born again won't have to suffer it because Jesus will pull them up from the earth and will—"

"Roxie—"

"I'm just explaining!"

"Okay," Glenna sighed, "go on."

"It's what happens at the end of the world. The idea is there's so much sin and corruption and crime and drugs and pornography and abortion and homosexuality—"

Glenna threw up her hands. "Just get to the point, Roxie," she said.

"I am. The world is going to have to pay for all that, except the saved ones, because the others will believe the false prophet who's going to appear and the apostate churches will support him—"

"Apostate churches?"

"Yes, the ones who have abandoned their true faith. And then the Beast and the false prophet will combine and there'll be persecution of the Jews again and then there'll be the Second Coming. Christ will come down and defeat the false prophet and the Beast—" She paused and studied Glenna's face. "What they believe is that the Bible says the Beast will arise in Russia and that Russia will attack Israel and that'll start the—"

"Enough," Glenna said. "I've got the picture. So what are you supposed to do about it?"

"Well, you try to get people to accept Christ in their hearts and live a Christian life . . ."

"Like a missionary?"

Roxie shrugged. "I guess."

"What about Jews?"

"Anyone can be born again. You just have to accept Christ."

"I see," Glenna said. "How much does it cost?"

"What?"

"How much does it cost? Has Daddy signed over the house to the church for after he dies? And all his worldly goods?"

"Oh, no . . ." Roxie thought about Kenny St. Pierre. "Daddy's not like that . . ."

"Anyone can be like that," Glenna said, "if they're scared enough and guilty enough and worried enough. Do they burn books?"

"No."

"Well, can you read what you want, then?"

Roxie looked sheepish. She hadn't planned to play devil's advocate, but she was making Glenna talk and Roxie had always seen things clearer after Glenna had talked to her.

"The thing is, you're not supposed to *want* to read—"

"Uh-*huh*." Glenna made a face. "Tell me," she said after a moment, "where *you* fit in."

"Nowhere, Glen!" Roxie wailed. "That's one of the reasons I've wanted to talk to you! I'm not sure how I feel. Daddy says it's all right to take what you're comfortable with and leave the rest, but that's not what the others seem to feel. The only one who's in the middle, like me, is Jarrell."

Glenna smiled and the tension Roxie had felt disappeared.

"Who's Jarrell?" she asked.

Roxie told her.

Glenna's homecoming was not the completely joyous occasion that all the Cables had expected. There were flare-ups and arguments.

"Mother," Glenna said, glaring at Marian, "Roxie is fifteen years old! Why can't she go to a movie with a boy, for heaven's sake? What is this 'soul-winning' business? What do you *mean* 'to make a plan is a mistake'? I don't understand you all. What's happened to my family, the one I've known for twenty-two years—where *are* you?"

"Calm down, honey. Now come on," Francis said, "don't exaggerate so." He took her hand and squeezed it. "The people down here are different from New York—"

"You don't have to tell *me* that!" Glenna shouted. "And *you're* different, too! I know I certainly wasn't so restricted when I was Roxie's age. You gave me freedom, you trusted my judgment—"

"Glenna Cable, you just watch the way you're speaking to us," Marian said sternly. "I'm not so sure I like the way you're behaving if this is the result of all that 'freedom' we gave you. If you're going to talk about changing, then let's talk about the way *you've* changed since you've been living by yourself in New York City."

"Oh, Mom!"

"Glenna, there's so much good to be drawn from the church," Marian said. "Really, there is. You'll see. Darling, we don't want to fight with you, we haven't seen you in so long—"

Glenna was near tears. "I don't want to fight with you, either, Mom . . . Daddy . . . I just worry about Roxie, that's all . . ."

"Roxie isn't unhappy, Glen," her father said and teased, "but I can't say I'm not worried about you, up there alone in Sin City."

"Oh, Daddy . . ."

They studied each other's faces as if they were seeing them for the first time.

"I love you!" Glenna blurted.

"Oh, Glen, we love you, too," her father said, hugging her.

The Pregers invited the Cables for a pre-Thanksgiving supper at their house so that they could all meet Glenna, who refused to go.

"I don't think I can keep my mouth shut," she said.

"Oh, Glenna," her mother moaned, "please! Now, these are our best friends. They're so anxious to meet you! Their daughter, Patty, the college girl, she'll be there—she wants to talk to you about New York . . ."

"I should tell her," Glenna said and rolled her eyes.

"Don't you dare!"

"Tell them I've got gonorrhea."

"Glenna!"

"Oh, say scurvy then, I don't care . . ."

"Glenna, you're twenty-two years old and you're behaving like a child! You can spend an evening with our friends and keep your opinions to yourself, like an adult with some control!"

"All right, I'll go, but I'm not making any promises!"

Though Marian felt a little ashamed of herself, she couldn't help worrying about Glenna—what she might say, how the Pregers might react.

"The Pregers won't mind Glenna's opinions, Mom," Roxie said. "You've heard Mrs. Preger argue with Daddy. She's so sure of what she believes he doesn't bother her with his questions. She always has an answer and she will for Glenna, too."

"Daddy doesn't argue with Cynthia Preger the way Glenna argues," Marian answered. "Glenna's young. She thinks she has all the answers. And it makes her sound hostile. Your father isn't hostile. I really wish I could have found some way to say no when Cynthia asked us over. I'm going to tell your sister—tell her to—"

"Cool it," Roxie finished.

"Exactly," Marian said.

Glenna wore her red suit to the Pregers'. Patty Preger spent fifteen minutes regaling its fashionable qualities, studying it carefully to see if she could copy it herself. Marian never imagined she'd be grateful to the House of Dior. Joe wanted to know about the buyers' training program in which Glenna was enrolled. And Cynthia wanted to know how and where Glenna furnished her apartment and where it was located because she'd been "up to New York once" in her early twenties and re-membered being frightened by its size and by the masses of people moving along its streets and sidewalks. Bess, not knowing exactly what to make of someone like Glenna, was unusually quiet.

It was Bess's feeling that everyone who actually lived in a place like New York City was one of those who chose to go his own independent way and therefore broke his fellowship with God. New York, to Bess, was full of sin, and she prayed that while Glenna was here, the Cables would try to help her find the true way.

Unaware of Bess's fervent prayers for her, Glenna smiled, nodded and answered questions.

During supper, Marian glanced with apprehension at Glenna each time Cynthia made reference to the Lord's leading her family to the Cables, or the Lord's giving Joe his wonderful business, or the Lord's plan for Patty's career or the Lord's showing her where she'd left her misplaced reading glasses. But Glenna's features remained calm and her demeanor unruffled.

By dessert, Marian began to relax.

"Have some cake, Glenna," Cynthia urged. "Surely you don't have to worry with such a lovely figure. And your mama made it."

"All right . . . Just a little, Mrs. Preger . . ."

"Aren't you just so proud of your mama? Why, look at how radiant she is! I declare, she's just bloomed since she came here to Howerton, don't you think so? It's the peace that comes when you know you've found the solutions!"

"Solutions?" Glenna raised her eyebrow. "It seems to me there are more problems than solutions . . ."

"Now, Glenna," Marian said quickly, "you've been

here such a short time and there's a lot you don't understand yet."

"That was a nice supper, Cynthia," Francis said, putting his coffee cup down.

"Sure was," Joe agreed. "Frank, why don't we go see if we can catch a ballgame on the TV while the girls clean up?" He pushed back his chair, rose and stretched.

"The girls?" Glenna said. "Come on, what is this? Dad always helps after meals. Don't you always tell us housework's an even deal, Daddy?"

But Cynthia said quickly. "This is how we do it in *our* house, Glenna, dear. Why, I just wouldn't be comfortable any other way."

Glenna's face flushed as Francis patted her on the shoulder and went into the living room with Joe. Bess and Roxie headed for the kitchen with Patty.

"Now, Glenna," her mother said, "don't make the rules for other people."

But Cynthia just nodded at Marian and smiled before turning to Glenna.

"Dear," she began, "I know you've been all by yourself up there in New York for several months. And during that time your family and ours have become quite close. Now, I see a lot of self-will in you and I surely do understand it. You know—in Romans—'For all have sinned, and come short of the glory of God'? We must bridge the gulf of that spiritual separation."

Glenna was silent.

"You know, a woman isn't supposed to be like a man," Cynthia continued. She leaned closer toward Glenna across the table. "Our Christian task is to teach a woman how to keep her womanliness. The womanly role is to give, Glenna. We all seem to have forgotten that."

"And the man's role is to take?" Glenna kept her voice even.

Cynthia smiled and leaned forward conspiratorially. "A man knows that women have been given the gift of intuition . . . special insights that men don't really possess. They feel a little inferior to us because of that. Our job is to support our men in all ways, so that they can support us. We complement each other the way man and woman should, not the way two equals would." She patted Glenna's hand.

Glenna took a deep breath. "Mrs. Preger," she said quietly, "so many strides have been made toward liberating women from old ideas . . . about how they couldn't take certain jobs or buy houses or earn as much as a man doing the same work. And changes like those have liberated men, too, because now they can share instead of having to be the only responsible ones in the family. Now men can—"

"Glenna, in Ephesians five, it is written: 'Wives, submit yourselves unto your own husbands, as unto the Lord. For the husband is the head of the wife, even as Christ is the head of the church: and He is the savior of the body. Therefore as the church is subject unto Christ, so let the wives be to their husbands in every thing.'"

"Number one, the Bible was written by men," Glenna said heatedly, "and number two, it was written in a different age, a long time ago, and number three, you can interpret portions of the Bible any way you want to make any point you want."

"My dear," Cynthia said, "there is only one way to

interpret the Bible and that is the way it was written. By the Lord Himself."

"By the *Lord Himself*?" Glenna looked at her mother standing silently at the end of the table. "Not by men? Prophets? Flesh and blood human beings?"

"By the Lord Himself, Glenna, my dear," Cynthia said, nodding. "Every word."

"Excuse me," Glenna said. "I think I'll go into the living room . . . If that's all right . . ."

Cynthia picked up the cups and saucers again. "Certainly, dear," she said brightly. "You go right ahead. Mercy, Marian, I'll bet the girls have everything done in the kitchen by now!"

Joe was muttering to himself as Glenna came in.

"Mmmm," she said, "I see there's growling in here, too. What are you watching?"

"Trying to watch some football," her father answered.

"But we can't get past this damn—this darn interference!" Joe added.

Jarrell came over as usual on Friday night. Roxie couldn't wait for Glenna to meet him. She didn't mind at all that she was hardly included in what was supposed to be a three-way conversation in the Cables' living room. She wanted her sister and Jarrell to get to know each other as well as they could so she could get the opinion of each about the other.

Jarrell stopped calling Glenna ma'am after the first ten minutes. He couldn't get enough of her stories about

New York. He asked her to describe streets, buildings—their outsides and insides, restaurants, nightclubs, the colors, the sense of excitement, all the things, Jarrell felt, that Howerton lacked.

With Glenna there, Jarrell told for the first time his ambitions to be a rock star. He told the secret with pride, but he made it known that he was trusting the sisters not to breathe a word about it.

"I've been taking lessons," he whispered, his eyes shining. "From a kid I know who goes to Marble Avenue. I can play almost anything I want now, even though I don't get to practice on account of I don't have my own guitar and can't take his home. But you should see how fast I've learned."

"He has a wonderful singing voice," Roxie told Glenna.

"Yeah, well, it's a different style from the hymns and spirituals . . ." Jarrell said. "But if I got me a white suit, cut like this"—he made a v-like slash across his chest—"with that sparkly stuff they sew on and real tight pants . . . 'Scuse me, but you know what I mean, like they wear for costumes—I got it all planned, I got it all planned . . . I swear, this is the first time I ever told anybody . . ."

Roxie fairly dragged Glenna up to her room after Jarrell had left.

"What did you think?" she asked, pulling on Glenna's arm. "Did you like him? Did you?"

Glenna smiled. "He's sweet," she said.

Roxie couldn't control her excitement. "What else? Tell me!"

"Oh, he's . . . he's . . . Oh, gosh, he reminds me so much of Harvey Wilmington . . . Remember him?"

"No . . ." Roxie didn't want to hear about Harvey Wilmington.

"He's that first boy I dated, don't you remember? Oh, well, you were little . . . He was so—I don't know, so *ardent*. Is that a silly word?"

"Glenna—"

"I'm sorry, Roxie. I liked him. He's nice. He's a nice boy. He's cute."

"Yes, but don't you think he's special? Different?"

"Well, he's different from the other boys you're likely to meet in this claustrophobic atmosphere. No, now don't get that look. Honey, all I mean is that you remind me of *me* at your age. The first love thing, where you get all starry-eyed and melty. It's very nostalgic for me. Jarrell is sweet, of course he is . . ."

Roxie clenched and unclenched her fingers.

"But tell me what you think about him," she begged Glenna. "Don't tell me about you at my age. We're different. This is now, this is me, this is Jarrell!"

Glenna sat down on the bed.

"Roxie, the only reason I mentioned Harvey Wilmington and me was because when you fall in love with someone for the first time—well, it's always the *same,* you see? I mean, Jarrell seems so special to you, but you should be meeting lots of boys, all different, so that you have some kind of choice. Up in New York, I could introduce you to ten boys, *twenty* boys, who all come from different backgrounds, with different ideas and—"

"I don't *care* about that!" Roxie cried, clapping her hands over her ears. "I just don't care about twenty other boys! You sound like Mom and Bess and Mrs. Preger and Mary Carol and—and—*nobody* tells me everything's okay! *Everybody* pushes me in a different direction all the time! Everybody says *this* is good for you and *that's* good for you and everybody's worried about everything I do and I thought you'd be different, but you're not and—I—" She stopped suddenly and flung herself down at the foot of her bed in a flood of tears.

Horrified, Glenna reached over and touched her, but Roxie curled herself into a little ball and cringed away.

"Oh, Roxie, don't," Glenna said, near tears herself. "Honey, I didn't mean to upset you, I didn't, I promise. I was only trying to show you—to tell you how I was feeling. Honest, I didn't mean to put more pressure on you, I didn't!"

"Go 'way," Roxie mumbled. Her arm was flung over her face. "Just leave me alone."

"I will . . ." Glenna stood up. "I will, but please forgive me, Rox. I wouldn't hurt you for anything . . ." She walked to the bedroom door. "Are you okay? I don't want to leave you like this . . ."

"I'm okay," Roxie said, not looking at her. "I just want to be by myself for a while."

Francis, working at his desk, looked up as Glenna stormed into his study and he drew in his breath at the sight of his daughter's red face and tight lips.

"Do you know what's happening to that girl up there?" Glenna said in a low voice. "Because *I* don't, Daddy. I don't know if Roxie is just being fifteen or if all this religious business is doing something to her, but she's so confused—she feels that everyone is pulling her in different directions—myself included, Daddy!"

"What kind of directions, what are you talking about?" Francis asked.

"I think that this church and these people are taking you over!" Her father opened his mouth, but she ran on. "No, I do, Daddy! And it scares me! You and Mom are all grown up and you've lived enough of life to decide what you want from the rest of it, whether I like it or not. But Roxie hasn't. And she's going to stifle here. Because according to Mrs. Preger and Mom, there's only one way of doing things and only one way of living. And no matter how hard it is out there, Daddy, and no matter how many mistakes I make, I'm going to find my own way of doing things and you're not giving Roxie that same opportunity!"

"Now wait," Francis said, holding up his hand. "Just wait a minute . . ." He sat back down in his chair. "I don't think you're being completely fair, Glen . . . Look, there are a lot of things about Stafford Hill that I don't know if I agree with . . . But there are many things that are quite worthwhile."

"Like what?"

"Like upholding and maintaining the family, that's what. Like focusing on traditional values and rising above the things that are happening out there, especially to the young people!"

"Well, I'm a young person!" Glenna shouted. "What about me? You gave me a good background and now I'm on my own. Don't you have faith in me?"

Francis hesitated.

"Well, *don't* you?"

He spread his hands. "I do—I love you, Glen—but I can't tell you that I don't worry about you . . . up there . . . Is that such a terrible thing? To worry about my daughter living alone in a big city?"

In the silence, they stared at each other.

"What are you thinking?" he asked finally.

"I'm wondering," she answered, looking away, "if I'm going to come down here again . . . for Christmas . . ."

Francis sighed. "I'm going upstairs to see if Roxie's all right," he said, and left the room.

Only when she was sure he had gone did Glenna allow herself to cry.

There were more tears as Marian and Roxie watched Glenna's plane take off, and even Francis was misty-eyed, but her visit had left everyone shaken.

"It's just Glenna. You know her ways," Francis said to his wife. "She was just being feisty—she needed to sound off."

"Oh, I know . . ." Marian said. "She'll calm down."

But Francis wasn't really worried about Glenna's calming down. He found the embers of his fear for his daughter enflamed by her intensity, and he was even more bothered by what effect a city like New York might have on her in time.

About Roxie, Francis wasn't as anxious as Glenna wanted him to be. Roxie was doing well in school. She had found a nice group of friends. Roxie was all right, her father decided.

Roxie felt she was all right, too. Despite Glenna.

A week after Thanksgiving, Jarrrell invited her to a party.

"Whose party?" Roxie asked.

"My friend Bill Wooster. The one I've been learning guitar from. He's having the party so his group can play and he said I can sit in. You can get to hear me with a group, Roxie. Your parents'll let you go, won't they? They're not like Bess Preger's parents or Louise Hawley's."

Roxie made a face. "A year ago they would have," she said. "Now I'm not so sure. About my mother, anyway . . ."

"Okay, then, tell them we're going out for dinner. Tell them we're going with Kenny and Kenny's married sister or something."

Roxie bit her lower lip.

"Anyway," Jarrell said with a grin, "Kenny does want to go with us. He wants to take Lee-Ann."

"*Kenny St. Pierre? And Lee-Ann?*"

"Sure. He likes her. What's wrong with Kenny?"

"Nothing. I'm just surprised, that's all. Does Lee-Ann know?"

"He wants you to tell her," Jarrell answered, still grinning.

"Let him tell her himself," Roxie said.

"He will, only he wants you to do it first. You know, break the ice. Because if she's really turned off, he better know it before he makes an—a fool out of himself."

Roxie shrugged. "Okay, I'll tell her."

"And if she says yes, your mother will be happy that you're going out with the 'right people,' right?"

"Kenny St. Pierre?" Lee-Ann cried.

Roxie giggled. "That's what *I* said," she told Lee-Ann. "But he's nice, don't you think?"

"I've known Kenny forever," Lee-Ann said. "He never even hinted at anything like that. Are you and Jarrell kidding me, Roxie? Because that's not really very nice . . ."

"I wouldn't do that to you, Lee-Ann. Do you really think I would? He likes you. Honest. But he's afraid you might not feel the same way. That's why he asked Jarrell to ask me to ask you! And there's a party next Saturday night that they want us to go to with them."

"Is Jarrell wild, Roxie?" Lee-Ann asked seriously. "There are stories about him and Kenny—well, you know, you've heard them. I mean—I know y'all like him and everything. I guess everybody knows that. Louise Hawley is jealous as anything even though she'd never say so. But Hope and Bess and I get a little worried about you. Has Bess said anything?"

Roxie shook her head. "She never talks about Jarrell at all. Bess and I study together at her house and my house but she doesn't ask me a thing about Jarrell."

"Well, I bet she'd like to. I wanted to, too, but I didn't want to seem nosy."

"We don't do anything bad, Lee-Ann," Roxie said.

"Are you chaperoned when you go out in a car?"

"We haven't gone out in a car. But we will this time if we go to this party . . . Bill Wooster and his date will pick us up and then go back to his house. Jarrell said I should tell my mother that we're going out for dinner at the Needham Hotel with Kenny and his married sister . . ." She looked carefully at Lee-Ann's face. "I don't like to lie, either. I never have," Roxie said. "And I may not. I'll just mention the party and I'll only lie a little bit if my mother says I can't go. Because I know she would have let me go if we still lived in Syracuse and she'd never met Mrs. Preger and Dr. Caraman and everything . . ."

Lee-Ann shifted from one foot to the other. "Well, I'd have to lie, that's for sure. There's no way my mother would let me go to some party that wasn't church-related . . . And I'm not too sure what she thinks of Kenny . . ."

"Well?" Roxie asked. "Would you go? If my mother knew you were going I know she'd let *me*."

Lee-Ann wrinkled her nose and smiled. "Does Kenny really like me?" she asked and giggled.

"Really. Really, he does. I wouldn't make that up. What are you laughing at?"

"Oh, nothing. It's just . . . well, why not? What's so awful about not having an adult in the car when you go out, anyway?"

"You say Lee-Ann is going, too?"

"Yes, Mo-ther . . ."

"And an adult will be along?"

"I really don't understand this third degree," Roxie said, folding her arms. "You never asked me any of these questions when we lived in Syracuse. And you know Jarrell. He's been sitting around this living room for- ever! We just want to do something a little different for a change!"

Francis intervened. "I think it'll be all right, Marian. We do know Jarrell, after all. It sounds like a perfectly nice date. And we wouldn't want Roxie to think we didn't trust her . . ."

"Of course I trust Roxie," Marian said stiffly. "It isn't that at all. It's outside influences I can't help worrying about."

Silence followed and Roxie stared at her mother.

"You'll be home by ten?" Marian asked.

"Eleven!"

"Roxie . . ."

"At *least* eleven. I'm fifteen years old!"

In Bill Wooster's car, Jarrell sat up front with Roxie, Lee-Ann and Kenny in the back seat.

"Did you have to lie?" Lee-Ann whispered to Roxie.

"I said we were having dinner at the Needham,"

Roxie said. "I didn't think I could say it was a Marble Avenue party. I really hated it, but I just can't believe my mother would get so up-tight. You'd think I was on my way to Hell, just going to a party!"

Lee-Ann sighed. "We're supposed to be turning away from temptation, Roxie. We're supposed to choose not to go."

"But I *don't* choose not to go," Roxie said petulantly.

Bill Wooster laughed. "You can lead a horse to water . . ."

". . . But you can't make him convert," Jarrell finished.

"Oh, stop it, Jarrell Meek. You're terrible," Lee-Ann said, but she smiled.

Bill's party was in his basement, which barely accommodated the crowd he'd invited. His four-piece group was playing loudly, but Roxie observed that no one seemed to mind. There were several cases of beer and when that ran out, someone went for more. Most of the kids were seniors at Marble Avenue, or older. They wore jeans and sweaters and they did a lot of dancing and laughing. Roxie and Lee-Ann felt overdressed in stockings and little heels. None of the four knew anyone except Bill, and when Jarrell went to sit in with the group, the other three clung together.

"Want a beer, Roxie?"

"No, thanks, Kenny. Jarrell's pretty good, isn't he?"

"Yeah. I didn't know he could play in a group like that. He said I'd be surprised and I am! Come on, have a beer, girls. Just one. Loosen up."

"No, I can't. My parents will smell it," Roxie said.

"I've got Tic-tacs. They won't smell it. Here." He picked up two cans and handed them to the girls. Lee-Ann opened hers, but didn't drink. Roxie sipped, decided it wasn't bad.

Jarrell motioned them closer. "Listen, listen to this," he mouthed as he began to play.

Roxie smiled at him. He looked so different playing and singing those songs instead of the hymns she was used to hearing. She wondered if he'd told Kenny about his ambition to be a musician. Lee-Ann poked her with her elbow and winked. Roxie grinned back. She drank some more of the beer and began to move to the rhythm.

Everyone seemed to enjoy Jarrell's singing and playing, so he stayed with the group, giving Roxie an occasional apologetic glance.

Roxie drank, bounced to the music, smiled at Jarrell and at Kenny, who was coaxing Lee-Ann to dance. But as the room became smokier and stuffier and the music louder, Roxie began to feel dizzy. Someone bumped her and she had trouble regaining her balance. She felt a trickle of perspiration at the back of her neck and suddenly knew she had to get out, get some fresh air. She struggled to reach the basement door and made it outside just in time.

She fell behind a bush, crouching on all fours, and lost her dinner and the beer under an upstairs window.

She hadn't heard Lee-Ann follow her out and when she sat up, breathing heavily, she saw her friend peering over the bush.

Roxie attempted a smile and shook her head.

"Y'all okay?" Lee-Ann asked nervously.

"Now I am . . ."

Lee-Ann opened her purse and handed Roxie a wad of tissues. "Come on," she said. "Let's go clean you up in the bathroom."

Roxie stood shakily, mopping her face.

"In a second," she said. "Let's stay here . . . just a second . . ."

"Okay . . ."

They moved to the front stoop and sat down.

"I guess I'm not a good drinker," Roxie said sheepishly. "I'm sorry to take you away from the party . . ."

"Oh, that's all right," Lee-Ann said. "It was getting too stuffy in there anyway."

They sat together in silence, breathing in the refreshing night air.

"Did you drink any beer?" Roxie asked after a while.

"Uh-uh."

"What are you thinking, Lee-Ann? Do you think I'm a terrible person?"

"Gosh, no, Roxie! I mean, I'm here, too, aren't I? I lied to my parents, too. And I don't think *I'm* a terrible person . . . I guess . . . Roxie?"

"What?"

"Do you think we'll be punished? God watches us all the time. Maybe being sick was your punishment."

"I hope so," Roxie said, "because I got it over with."

"Oooh, then mine is yet to come," Lee-Ann said.

"Listen," Roxie said, "my sister is worried that I won't learn to think for myself. Well, I can, and what I think is that I learned I can't drink very much or I'll get sick. So I've been taught something that's good. And that means I'm not a terrible person, right?"

"I don't think Dr. Caraman would see it that way," Lee-Ann said with a sigh. "Ephesians says, 'Children, obey your parents in the Lord: for this is right.'"

"I know," Roxie countered, "but it also says, 'And, ye fathers, provoke not your children to wrath,' doesn't it?" She stuck out her tongue playfully at Lee-Ann, who laughed and clapped her hands.

Back inside, they found a bathroom and Roxie washed her face and hands. There was also a small bottle half-filled with mouthwash in the medicine cabinet and she used it up.

Feeling tired, but presentable, she and Lee-Ann descended the basement stairs, where the boys rushed over to them.

"Are you okay?" Jarrell asked, studying her.

"Were you sick?" Kenny wanted to know.

Roxie nodded. "I was—Lee-Ann was just helping me. But I'm okay now."

"Sure?" Jarrell took her hand. "I'm sorry I left you for so long. I won't do that again." He turned to Kenny. "She's not used to beer. You shouldn't have given her any."

"I'm sorry," Kenny said. "I'm real sorry. Honest." He looked at Lee-Ann. "Honest, Lee-Ann."

"It's okay, Kenny," Roxie said. "It wasn't your fault. But do you think Bill would mind driving us home now?"

Louise Hawley cornered Roxie in home economics.

"I know you're going out with Jarrell," she said. "I'm surprised your parents let you."

Roxie's mouth opened but she couldn't find any words.

"I pray for you, Roxie. I just want you to know that. I'd hate for you to move out of the sphere of righteousness."

Angered, Roxie found her tongue. "I'm not doing anything wrong, Louise, and I don't see where it's your business what I do, anyway!"

"It's only because your friends care about you," Louise said peevishly. "After all, it's nothing to me personally!"

Try as she might, Roxie couldn't shake the feeling of guilt. In her heart, she felt her actions were in no way sinful. A year before she would have told her parents, not only about going to a party, but about having drunk too much and having learned a lesson. Her mother would have just scolded and frowned and her father would have laughed. That would have been all. Now, she couldn't tell them anything.

"It's not the fear of displeasing God," she told Lee-Ann, "it's the fear of displeasing my parents!"

And then, Glenna's letter arrived.

"Oh, Francis, I can't believe we won't all be together at Christmas," Marian said. Her voice was soft and it stabbed at Roxie.

"I know, hon, I know . . ." Francis put his arm around her shoulder.

"It's not going to be the same, that's all. It just won't be the same."

"It won't be the same," Roxie said, "but we can try to make it nice—the three of us . . . Right? Right, Daddy?"

"Sure. Of course we will, honey."

She couldn't bear the hurt in her parents' eyes. She went to her room and closed the door.

Oh, Glenna, she thought, I will miss you, I will.

But part of her was afraid of more scenes with her sister and their parents and she wanted desperately to avoid that. She wanted her sister to be proud of her and she wasn't sure that Glenna would understand that she was thinking for herself but she was keeping peace at home, too.

Now Glenna wasn't coming. And Roxie felt guilty about her relief. She had to write to her sister and tell her immediately how disappointed she was.

Dear Glen,

I can't believe you won't be with us at Christmas. Mom and Dad are heartbroken as you can imagine, but I guess we understand about Caroline. If you're the only one she's got to be with her at her wedding then I guess you have to be there, except I agree with you that six weeks isn't very long to know someone before you marry him. Maybe they will let you off from work to come home after Christmas if you ask them. Maybe for New Year's?

I'm sorry I haven't written since Thanksgiving and I'm sorry about our fight. I think we should call a truce because I don't think that you completely understand me right now but I love you, so I hope you let me work things out by myself for a while.

This is something I haven't told Mom or Daddy so please don't mention anything about it when you write or talk to them. But I want you to know, so maybe you will see that I really know what I'm doing.

I've been going out with Jarrell and I haven't told the whole truth about where we go and who's with us. Part of me feels very guilty about that and part of me doesn't. It's hard to explain. But we don't do anything bad. Once I drank too much beer at a party and got sick, but I thought of what you said about making mistakes so you could learn from them and I did learn from that. So I really am all right.

I also hope that things are all right between you and me. Please tell Caroline good luck from us.

Love,
Roxie

Roxie looked at the clock. It had taken her over an hour to write her letter. She wanted each word to be just right. She read it four times straight through, to be sure.

XII

It was a few days later when Roxie and Bess, bursting into the kitchen on a break from their homework, found Marian alone at the table with her head on her arms.

"Mom?" Roxie said, sliding into the seat opposite her mother. "Are you okay?" She reached out and touched Marian's hand.

Marian sat up. "Sure, honey, sure I am. Just tired, that's all."

"Can I get you something, Mrs. Cable?" Bess asked. "Some ice water?"

"Thank you, Bess, I'm fine. Just gathering my strength. I'm going out to witness tonight. First time by myself . . ." She smiled.

"Where to?" Bess asked.

"A young boy. Seems to be all alone in the world. He's in the hospital with a badly cut eye and three broken ribs. He won't say how it happened. All he said was that he's in the Navy . . . but not how he ended up here in Howerton." She smiled up at Bess. "Your mother thinks he'd be a good starting point for me. I've always gone with her or Olivia Heffernan before . . ."

Roxie looked at her mother's face. She didn't think Marian was tired. Marian never got tired. But ever since Glenna wrote that she wouldn't be home for Christmas, her mother's face had looked worn. Roxie frowned. Her sister was making everyone feel bad . . . Roxie felt angry with her again.

"I'll go with you, Mom!" Roxie said suddenly.

Marian sat up and stared. Her whole face seemed to relax. She smiled at Roxie. "Will you? Will you, really, dear?"

"Oh, Roxie, what a good idea!" Bess cried. "You'll be wonderful, I know it. You have such a friendly way with people?" The upturned inflection, Roxie thought. Like her mother.

"Sure. I'd like to go with you."

Marian beamed at her daughter and squeezed her hand. "Oh, Roxie," she said, "that would mean so much to me."

The young man's head was turned toward the wall and all Marian and Roxie could see was a thick bandage that covered his left eye and half his face.

Marian pulled a chair up next to his bed and Roxie stood behind it, working her fingers nervously on its backrest.

"Edward?" Marian whispered.

The boy did not move.

Marian shifted in her chair.

"Edward?" she said again, after a moment. "We've come to visit you for a bit . . ."

There was still no response, but Marian continued. "My name is Mrs. Cable. Marian Cable. You may call me Marian, if you like . . ."

The boy didn't turn his head.

"Maybe he's asleep," Roxie whispered, leaning over the back of the chair.

Marian shook her head and went on.

"There's a young, pretty girl with me," she said lightly. Roxie clicked her tongue and looked away. "She's my daughter, Roseanne. She goes to high school here in Howerton. She's come to visit, too. Wouldn't you like to turn and look at us?"

The boy, Edward, moved his legs slightly, but kept his face to the wall.

"I guess you're in a lot of pain, Edward," Marian said softly. "I'm so sorry. Won't you tell us how it happened?"

"He doesn't want to talk, Mom," Roxie whispered, but still her mother persisted.

"Edward, I don't know how your . . . accident happened, but perhaps there will come a day when you see it as a turning point in your life. From this pain can come your greatest joy."

Slowly, the boy turned his head. The unbandaged half of his face was discolored and Roxie couldn't help wincing at the sight of exposed stitches near his ear.

"Go 'way," he managed, and closed his good eye. "Please."

"Just listen for a moment, Edward," Marian said.

Roxie clutched the back of her mother's chair even tighter until her knuckles were white and her fingers ached.

"You're a special person, Edward," Marian continued. "A lot of people you don't even know are worried about you. Like me. And my daughter. And others, too. We want very badly for you to get well . . . and begin a brand new life. It can be a life of joy, Edward."

"Please . . ." the boy mumbled.

"Edward, listen. The Lord's ways are strange. In the Bible—James—'My brethren, count it all joy when ye fall into divers temptations.' These testings were sent to you by the Lord, Edward. Edward? Were you brought up in a religious home?"

The boy nodded once. Slowly.

"Catholic?" Marian asked. His head moved to the right. "Protestant?" A nod. "Did you . . . Did you ever feel—during your religious upbringing—that you had a personal, intimate relationship with Jesus?"

The boy closed his good eye and exhaled. "No," he whispered and twisted his mouth. "Religion never meant much to me."

Marian leaned forward. "Well, that's the difference," she said almost triumphantly. "It can't mean very much to you unless you know that Jesus is actually there, right with you, Edward. Not far away, not only in church, but right there, next to your bed, watching you, guiding you every step of the way . . . And you'll see Him, Edward . . . You'll know it if you only open your spiritual eyes to Him. It's true, Edward." She looked over her shoulder. "Isn't it, Roxie?" she asked, but she didn't wait for Roxie's answer.

"I know you're tired, Edward," she said, lightly touching his arm. "I'm going to let you rest now. But I want to come back very much. And I'll read to you, all right? Passages from the Bible that I know you'll feel so personally! Would that be all right?" She waited, but Edward's eye was closed and he didn't answer. "All right, Edward," Marian said, as if he had. "I'll see you again. You're going to get stronger every day. Goodbye, Edward . . ."

She got up and tiptoed toward the door with Roxie at her heels. Once outside, she leaned against the tiled wall and sighed. "Whew," she breathed, and smiled at Roxie. "How'd I do? Do you think I made an impression?"

Roxie twisted her lip. "I don't know," she said. "Mom? Did you really believe what you were saying in there? Did you really believe that his accident or whatever it was could be *joyful?* And that everything would be all right if he just thought Jesus was standing next to his bed? Did you, Mom?" She frowned. "Because I never heard you talk that way before. Mrs. Preger talks that way all the time, but you don't. At least not to me . . ."

Marian sighed again.

"Well, that's what witnessing is, Roxie. You try to turn the people to God and away from sin." She took Roxie's arm and they began to walk down the corridor toward the elevator. "The feeling is that that boy was in a knife fight. And that the fight was over drugs. Now if he can be turned away from living that kind of life, from being involved with things like that, by becoming involved with God instead, now is there anything wrong with that?"

"Well, but why can't you just say that you care about him? Maybe nobody ever cared about him before. Maybe that would make a difference. I mean, somebody he doesn't even know caring about him. Why couldn't you read him some good stories or something? Why does it have to be the Bible?"

The elevator arrived and they squeezed in with a crowd of visitors.

"Because," Marian said softly, "I won't be a permanent part of his life. And if he turns to Jesus and the Bible, he'll have those always. To turn to. And if he gets saved, then his whole life will be different. He won't get into knife fights ever again. That very thing happened to one of the pastors at Stafford Hill. Did you know that?"

They walked off the elevator with Marian's hand still circling Roxie's arm. Now she squeezed it.

"It meant a lot to me, having you there," she said. "I'm proud of you. It was hard looking at that badly bruised face, wasn't it? Poor boy . . ."

Roxie looked at the floor. "Well, you were nice to him, Mom. You spoke so gently . . . Are you going back?"

"Of course!"

As Christmas drew nearer, Roxie made more of it than she ever had, as if her fussing and caring would fill Glenna's empty place.

"Isn't it funny to have Christmas with no snow?" she asked, arranging a wreath in the living room window.

"And no cold!" Marian said. "I love it."

"Back home we'd be plowing through twelve-foot drifts!" Roxie laughed. "This is so weird!"

"How much snow is there?" Francis asked. "Have you heard from Ellie lately?"

"No . . . But I got a postcard from Peter. From Florida!"

"Oh, well, he wouldn't know then, lucky boy."

"Are we going on a vacation, too?" Roxie asked. "I don't mean now, of course . . ."

"Oh, boy, not now is right," her father breathed. "I've practically just started work here and I'm swamped. Besides . . ." He stopped, made a face and picked up his paper.

"Besides what?"

"Besides, vacations are expensive," Marian finished.

"That's right. Even Christmas is going to be much less of the extravagant affair we've always made of it," Francis added. He looked up at Roxie. "Sorry, baby. Just don't have the cash this year."

"We donated a lot to the church ministries," Marian said. "We felt it was more important to share with others."

"This is cashmere," Marian said, running her fingers over her new beige pullover. "Feel it, Roxie. Isn't it soft?"

"Uh-huh . . ." She wondered if her mother really liked the plaid blouse she had bought her at Milly's—it wasn't nearly as fancy as this cashmere sweater Glenna had sent.

"And look what she chose for you, Roxie! A quilted vest—it's so different! Look at the colors!"

"It'll probably be too hot," Roxie said.

"Oh, no, it won't. It'll be perfect." She looked at Francis admiring his deerskin slippers. "We should call her, Frank," she said. "Right now, don't you think?"

"Yes, of course. How about it, Rox?"

"Uh-huh."

"Want to talk first?"

"No, you first, Daddy . . ."

Glenna sounded bubbly.

"Did you really like them? I shopped so long for just the right things! Oh, and thank you for mine! Everything fits perfectly!" She had spent Christmas eve at a dinner party given for Caroline and her fiancé by his parents. It was lovely, their tree was gorgeous, it *had* snowed in New York but it was all just slush now, she missed them very much.

"We miss you, too, honey, more than I can tell you," Marian said. She didn't ask if Glenna had been to church. "Would you—uh—like to talk to your sister now?"

"Sure!"

Roxie got on and made her voice bright.

"Thanks for the vest, Glen. It's pretty!"

"As soon as I saw it, I thought of you, babe! How—um—how are you?"

"Fine . . ."

"I liked your letter . . . I haven't had a chance to answer it yet, but I will. I've been going crazy with this wedding . . ."

"I know, I've been busy, too."

"How's Jarrell?"

"He's fine."

"Still the big thing?"

"Yes . . ."

"Listen, you asked about New Year's—I wish I could, but I absolutely can't get away. The job is wackier than ever. Maybe later in January, though. Or early February . . . Are you really okay, Rox?"

"Uh-huh."

"Mom?"

"She's fine. Daddy, too. We're all fine . . ."

The call made Roxie uncomfortable. It was the first time she could remember being uncomfortable talking to Glenna. But she had the feeling Glenna felt the same way.

Roxie caught herself rationalizing her behavior that vacation. Feeling for the first time in her life that she couldn't confide in her mother, she stretched the truth, as she called it. If she and Jarrell went to the movies in Annenville with Kenny and Lee-Ann, Roxie told Marian they were all working on a club project; if they went to a rock concert with Bill Wooster, she implied that they were attending a recital, or a musicale.

It all made her uncomfortable, but she felt an unidentified pressure that forced her to be calculating.

She was especially unhappy about her relationship with Bess. Because she was feeling so defensive, Roxie was sharp when Bess asked questions which stemmed only from Bess's concern for her friend.

"I guess you go to a lot of parties with the Marble Avenue kids," Bess said one evening when she and Roxie were together.

"Not a lot. Anyway, they're nice kids."

"Do they drink at them? The parties?"

"No."

"Are their parents home?"

"Sure."

"I'll bet . . ."

"Come on, Bess, don't pick at me!"

"I'm not, Roxie. I worry about you. And I pray for you. Everybody knows about you and Jarrell Meek. And Kenny St. Pierre and Lee-Ann, too."

"So what!"

"It's just that I've known Lee-Ann practically all my life and I know she's a good Christian girl. But you're new to the church, Roxie, and sometimes it's hard for new converts. There are people who say that going out with you really reformed Jarrell. They say how much more righteous he is and how he joined Youthlight and everything . . ."

"So?"

"But other people say it's just the other way around. That he's leading you down the wrong path and you're the one who's getting just like *him*."

"Look, Bess, I don't know who all these people are who find so much time to talk about me. Why don't we just have a trial and a jury and then all these 'people' can get in on it and a judge can make a decision! Honestly!" Roxie snapped. "It makes me sick sometimes!" She felt sick right then as she looked into Bess's concerned eyes.

"I'm just trying to be your friend," Bess said quietly.

"Well, be my friend then, and not my conscience!"

XIII

Roxie's invitation to the Pregers' New Year's Eve party did not come from Bess, but from her own parents, who were also invited, along with the Heffernans from down the street, the Hawleys and some of Joe and Cynthia's other friends. Though the party was officially for the Pregers' daughters, Cynthia thought the adults might enjoy a party of their own while chaperoning the young people.

"But I want to go to another party," Roxie told her mother. She and Jarrell had already made plans.

"But, honey, it's the Pregers! Besides, this way we'll all be together as a family on New Year's. That's so important to me this holiday, Roxie. Isn't it to you?"

Roxie thought about Glenna and said, "Yes, Mom . . . Sure it is."

"Besides," Marian went on, "it's such a dangerous night, New Year's Eve, and there are people who have too much to drink and do reckless things . . ."

"It's okay, Mom . . ." Roxie said.

Marian softened. "I guess you would like to spend the evening with Jarrell, wouldn't you?"

Roxie nodded.

"Well, perhaps Bess will ask him."

She might if I talked her into it, Roxie thought, but she won't be thrilled about it. And neither will he.

"Jarrell?" Cynthia asked. "And Kenny St. Pierre, too?"

"Yes," Bess answered. "I thought I should ask them. For Roxie and Lee-Ann."

"Did the girls ask you to invite them?"

"No, Roxie only asked me if I had, she didn't ask me if I *would*. But I want to. I know the girls will be happier, and besides, I really don't mind Jarrell Meek a lot of the time. Whenever I see him he's always polite and funny . . ."

"Well," Cynthia said, "it is yours and Patty's party. I just hope you know what you're doing, but all of us adults will be around to make sure everything's all right . . ."

"Yes . . . I'm sure it'll be all right, Mama," Bess said.

Wanda Hawley glared at her daughter, Louise.

"Of course you're going, I never heard such a thing, Louise Hawley," she said, her arms folded across her chest.

"I don't mind staying home by myself on New Year's, Mama," Louise said. "I just don't want to go to the party, that's all."

"Now, I just don't understand you," Wanda said

crossly. "All your friends are going to be there . . . Why on earth would you want to sit home all by your lonesome? You like Bess Preger and all those other boys and girls from school . . ."

"Not all of them," Louise said.

"What are you talking about?" Wanda demanded.

"Just that I don't necessarily like all of the people Bess invited, that's all."

"I frankly think the Pregers and everyone else will be right disappointed if you don't go, after they've been kind enough to invite us all. Your daddy and I are surely going. Now just because you may have had a little tiff with someone doesn't mean—"

"I haven't had a 'little tiff,' Mama," Louise interrupted. "I just—I—" She closed her eyes and saw Jarrell Meek's smile. But the smile wasn't for her. Even in her imagination, Jarrell was smiling at Roxie.

"Louise? Are you sick?" Wanda asked, peering at her daughter.

"No, Mama, I'm not sick."

"You going to this party or not, Louise Hawley? Now I want the right answer out of you."

"Yes, Mama, I'm going. I'll go, Mama," Louise answered. She sighed. She knew all along she'd be going to the Pregers' party. She wondered why she'd fussed about it in the first place.

The party divided itself into three groups—Patty's college friends, Bess's high school friends and the adults. No alcoholic beverages were served, but there was plenty of food.

"Where's Jarrell?" Hope whispered to Roxie. "I heard he was coming. And I also heard Louise almost didn't come. But there she is, standing next to her father . . ."

"Jarrell will be here," Roxie said casually, but she was worried. He was forty-five minutes late.

"Kenny, too?" Hope asked.

"Uh-huh, I think so . . ."

"Well, I'm glad," Hope said. "I think they're fun, no matter how much Louise Hawley carries on about their wildness. They'll put a little life into the party when they arrive, I'll bet."

Roxie gave Hope a grateful look.

The boys were an hour and ten minutes late. Roxie had checked her watch every five minutes. Her heart leaped when she saw them at the door and it instantly sank when she got a good look at them. Kenny's tie was loose. Jarrell had a silly grin on his face.

They tried to carry it off—at least, Jarrell did. He explained politely that Kenny hadn't been feeling too well so they had stopped at the 7-Eleven to get medicine, but during this recital, Kenny happened to catch Jarrell's eye and the two of them burst into uproarious laughter.

"You big jerk," Lee-Ann whispered, elbowing Kenny in the ribs. "You probably just spoiled everything. Even if Mr. and Mrs. Cable didn't see you, just look over there!"

Kenny looked. Bess and Louise Hawley were standing at the food table, talking to each other in hushed voices and glowering at the boys.

"Oh, my father isn't glad today!" Jarrell moaned and Roxie couldn't help smiling. Bess and Louise weren't at all amused.

Jarrell and Kenny managed not to stumble or spill anything. They were polite, even if their words were slightly slurred, and Jarrell's southern accent sounded thicker than usual. They told a very long joke, the punch line of which was greeted with stony silence by everyone within hearing except for two Christian Grace College boys who snorted loudly.

In the silence, Louise walked over to Jarrell.

"That was just disgusting, Jarrell Meek," she said. "And you have been drinking, you and your stupid, vulgar friend."

Jarrell drew himself up. "When I want your opinion, Miss Hawley, I will"—he burped loudly—"ask for it!"

Kenny laughed so hard he had to leave the room.

"Dis-gusting!" Louise cried, near tears. "I will not stay and see you embarrass nice people like the Pregers with your vile behavior—" Louise turned quickly and ran to the little guest room to get her jacket, shaking off her father's hand as he reached out to stop her.

Roxie and Lee-Ann gripped each other's arms tightly, watching the faces of the party guests, rather than Jarrell's.

"Oh, Roxie," Lee-Ann said, her eyes wide. "If my parents were here, they'd just die . . ."

Louise reappeared from the guest room wearing her white linen jacket. The crowd had become noisy again and Roxie couldn't hear the conversation Lew Hawley was having with his daughter at the back door. But she did see Louise leave, and slam the door behind her.

As Kenny also reappeared from the downstairs bathroom, Jarrell grabbed him by the shoulder and went over to Roxie's parents.

"Kenny and I are going to leave now, Mr. Cable, Mrs. Cable . . . I want you to know that we're awful sorry for our bad behavior tonight. We got real silly. You know, happy over the New Year and all that. And if we embarrassed you and Roxie we apologize again. Uh . . . hope you don't hold it against me . . ." He glanced at Roxie as he finished his speech and then dragged Kenny over so that he could repeat it to the Pregers.

"Don't go, Jarrell," Roxie said as the boys walked toward the door together. "Stay and cool down a little."

"That's right, if you leave now, it'll just look worse for you," Lee-Ann said.

"I'm sorry, Lee-Ann, I didn't mean for us to get so—happy," Kenny said. His face was red and Lee-Ann couldn't tell if it was due to blushing or beer. "But—we better go. Look around."

The girls looked. The college crowd was amusing itself, but the Stafford Hill group was staring at the two couples.

Jarrell opened the front door. "Happy New Year, Roxie," he said.

Three blocks away, Louise Hawley leaned against a lamppost, panting. She had run all the way from the

Pregers'—run blindly, not even caring in which direction she was headed. The scene Jarrell had made—the scene she herself had made—was causing her actual physical pain.

Only when she reached this corner, where the residential section virtually stopped and the fields and mountains stretched before her, did she allow herself to stop running.

" 'Put away from three a froward mouth, and perverse lips put far from thee,' " she murmured to herself. Then: "How could they do it? How could they?"

She began to cry. Tears rolled down her hot cheeks. She dug her fingernails into her palms. I won't cry, she thought. Why should I cry? " 'Blessings are upon the head of the just: but violence covereth the mouth of the wicked' . . ."

A car filled with celebrating teen-agers careened past her, heading toward the farms. She started at the sounds of the screams and laughter of the young passengers. They reminded her that she was still in Howerton, not in a deserted country spot—and that it was still New Year's Eve. She looked around, feeling she had to go somewhere, do something . . .

She pushed herself away from the lamppost and considered her options. The party was out; she'd never go back there. A walk wouldn't help. She was too tired, anyway.

"I guess I'll just go home," she said aloud. A couple walking across the street turned and looked at her.

She noticed more people on the street and her stomach began to flutter at the thought that all of them were watching her, staring at her. She looked wildly around for someplace to go where she could breathe and feel alone.

"Did you say anything to Jarrell after he apologized?" Roxie asked her father when they got home.

"No, he didn't give us a chance."

"I was just shocked at his behavior," Marian said. "Really, I was. He's always been such a perfect gentleman."

"He is, Mom. He just made a mistake."

"He certainly did. At least he had the decency to leave when he did. It's too bad the Hawley girl went off by herself."

"Lew wanted to go with her," Francis said, "but she wouldn't let him. She said she wanted to go home alone."

"Do you think she'll be all right?" Marian asked.

"Oh, she'll be all right," Roxie said. "She just wanted to make a scene and show everybody how good she is and how bad Jarrell is. It's only because she likes him so much. She couldn't stand to see him with me."

"Roxie! Louise isn't like that."

"Louise is exactly like that. She sniffs at me in the halls at school."

Francis laughed. "She *sniffs?*" he said.

Roxie began to smile. "She does, Daddy. She goes 'hmmmmph'!"

"Sounds like she's got a sinus condition," Francis joked.

"Jarrell really wasn't drinking, was he, Roxie?"

"Oh, Mom, can't we just forget it? Please?"

"You don't drink with him, do you?"

"I don't drink, Mom."

"Oh, Jarrell's all right," Francis said. "Maybe he was just nervous tonight. I can understand that. He's not the type to go and do somthing to deliberately embarrass people like the Pregers or you, Roxie. Anyway, he apologized, so why don't we just forget it?"

"Yes, let's," Roxie said. The last thing she wanted to do was talk about Jarrell with her mother. She had felt embarrassed, and threatened, too, by Jarrell's behavior.

"Joe and Cynthia did a good job with that mixed crowd," Francis was saying. "The college kids were nice, didn't you think, Marian?"

Roxie didn't hear her mother's reply. She was picturing Bess Preger's face when they said good night.

"Happy New Year, Bess," Roxie had said. Then, casually, "I'm sorry about Jarrell and Kenny and Louise and all that. But it was a nice party anyway . . ."

Bess blinked at her. "Y'all have a happy new year, too, Roxie," she'd said, and quickly turned back into the room.

New Year's Day was a Sunday, and the Stafford Hill church was filled as usual.

"Well, of course," Francis whispered to his wife. "No one here has any hangover!"

Or if they do, they don't show it, Roxie thought, watching Kenny St. Pierre, in tie and jacket, enter the church with his parents. She couldn't find Jarrell, but she knew he'd be there.

"Have you cleaned up from your party?" Marian asked Cynthia Preger. Cynthia looked spry and trim in her navy blue suit and white blouse.

"Oh, yes, last night. Patty and Bess helped with everything. It was fun, wasn't it? I mean, in spite of that little scene with the boys . . ."

"It was very nice," Marian said.

"I saw the Hawleys in the parking lot just now. Wanda says Louise was home when they got back last night. She seemed all right this morning . . . Thanked me for the party. I was rather embarrassed since it was obvious she didn't have a very good time . . ."

"Well, we did, Cynthia," Marian assured her.

"Good . . . Marian, Bess has told me Roxie sees a good deal of the Meek boy. Do you think that's all right?"

Now Marian wasn't quite sure how all right it was, but she said defensively, "Oh, Jarrell has always been a perfect gentleman at our house. You know how teen-age boys are when they get in a crowd, trying to be big men—that kind of thing . . ."

Cynthia's lips tightened. "Yes, I know teen-age boys," she said stiffly.

Marian went on quickly, "He just thinks the world of Roxie, the way he treats her, he—" She broke off as Dr. Caraman himself stepped forward to begin the service. This was unusual. As a general rule, one of the pastors began by reading a passage of the Bible and there was always a hymn sung before Dr. Caraman came, smiling, to the pulpit. He was not smiling now.

"Welcome, everyone," he said—a half-smile, now—"to the Stafford Hill Baptist Church on this, the first day of a brand new year. I want to address you—" He stopped, looked down. "I wanted to share only good tidings with you on this day, but I'm afraid something has happened to change that."

Marian looked at Francis, who raised his eyebrows questioningly.

"Last night, New Year's Eve, as you all know . . . Well, sometime during the night, part of our transmitting tower and the antenna on top of it—at the edge of town on the hill—was deliberately knocked to the ground." There was a gasp from his audience. "Yes, my friends, it was deliberate. You will read about it in your papers today or tomorrow. This destruction was not due to weather conditions—it was a lovely night, I sincerely hope it was a lovely night for all of you—" He smiled, but only briefly. "This was vandalism, caused by human hands, not God's. I'm not at liberty to say how we know this right now, but we do."

The congregation shifted in the pews. Roxie looked over at her mother, but Marian and Cynthia were shaking their heads at each other.

"Now I don't like to bring my troubles to my flock," Dr. Caraman continued. "And yes, my friends, we do have troubles. There are many who would like to see all our good work destroyed, who would like to see me, personally, destroyed . . . I don't tell you these things. I don't tell you about the letters I get, the letters, the abuse, the threats, no, I don't bring these things into church because I'm not a complainer, I'm not a whiner and I'm not a quitter! I've talked with the Lord, I've talked with Him many times, and no, I'm not afraid. I get discouraged. Yes, I do get discouraged. I'm weak,

I'm human, but, my friends, I know the work I must do and I'm prepared to do it, for the *Lord* and not for *myself!*"

Someone cried, "That's right!"

"Yes," Dr. Caraman went on, "I know you're all my devoted friends. I know you're all personal friends of Jesus Christ. I know how each of you must feel hearing about this terrible crime against Him and all our work in His name. And, my friends, there will be revenge against this crime!"

A woman cried, "Amen!"

"But, my friends, it is not *our* job to get revenge!"

Someone in a front pew cried, "No!"

"No!" Dr. Caraman echoed. "No, it is not our job. It is *God's* job! God wants His word transmitted, wants His word sent out on all those radio stations and all those television stations to all those people out there who are *waiting for it!*" He took a breath and continued. "Those who try to halt the spread of the word of God will be punished. But by *Him*. Not by us! We do not have to worry!

"Sometimes when I am traveling, up there in our airplane, en route to a place where there are lost souls reaching out for the word of God through the power of the Holy Spirit—even though I am far above the earth, far away from that ground below, somewhere—a hundred or so miles away—*somewhere,* someone has our little craft on a marvelous invention called radar. Someone I don't know is watching me at that very moment, even though I am miles and miles away from him and above the earth. That fact has never ceased to amaze me.

Someone in some little airport so far away, tracks *me*, knows where *I* am.

"Do you see what I'm getting at, my friends?

"Although those vandals were sure there wasn't a soul in sight when they performed their work, they *were* on a radar screen *somewhere!*"

"Ah!" someone breathed.

"God's radar screen!" Dr. Caraman bellowed. "They were on *God's* radar screen all the time they thought no one was watching. They were on God's radar screen—all—the—time.

"Let us pray that God will show *us* what He saw on His radar screen last night." He looked down at the pulpit and there was silence throughout the church.

"And now," he said, "I'd like to hear from our wonderful Christian Grace Choir, lifting their voices to the Lord."

Roxie played with her fingers in her lap as the choir began to sing. She looked over at Bess, two seats away, but Bess was staring at her sister, Patty, in the choir, the way she always did when the choir sang.

Roxie decided it was all right to look around. She spotted the Hawleys and the Seeds to her left across the aisle. She couldn't see Louise, but she did see Molly Seeds take little Diane from their father's lap and put her on her own.

Roxie craned her neck until she finally saw Jarrell.

He was seated ahead of her by several rows, between his father and his mother. Roxie sat back. She'd found him, that was enough. She didn't want to attract his attention. She was hurt. He had blown it! Just when she'd needed him to behave well in front of all those church people and her parents, he went and got drunk and acted like an idiot. Louise will have a field day out of it, she thought. She stopped staring at the back of his head. Someone had once told her that if you stared at someone long enough you could make him turn around, and she decided not to test it.

"Some business, eh?" Joe Preger said when they were all outside. "How do you s'pose that happened?"

"You mean the antenna?" Francis asked. "Yeah. Well, I sure know who it was."

"Frank! *Do* you?" Cynthia asked. Her eyes were wide. "Honest?"

"Sure! A couple of hot sports fans who wanted a clear picture for the bowl games this afternoon!"

"Oh, Francis," Marian said. "You really scared me for a minute."

"It's like defiling the church," Cynthia said. "It's the Lord's tower."

"You think that's why they did it, Frank?" Joe asked seriously. "Because of the reception?"

"Oh, I don't know, Joe. It popped into my mind because there's such interference when it's used, that's all. I mean," he laughed, "that's why *I'd* do it!"

"Francis, don't even joke about something like that," Marian said.

"Besides, we know where you were last night," Cynthia teased. "And you, too, Joe."

"Well, how about watching the games at our house,

Frank?" Joe suggested. "And you girls are invited, too, of course, right, hon?"

"Oh, right, honey. Why, I've got so much food left over from the party, we'll just never finish it if you folks don't help, now will we, Bess?"

Roxie looked at Bess, who wouldn't look back, just shook her head. "No, Mama, we won't," she answered softly.

The reception was "clear as a bell," as Joe Preger conceded. Roxie, who hated football, found herself watching both the Cotton Bowl and the Sugar Bowl as the men, grunting and cheering, kept switching channels. She tried to help in the kitchen, but with Marian, Cynthia, Bess and Patty all taking care of the food, she was just in the way. Bess barely spoke to her.

The Heffernans dropped in and so did the Hawleys—without Louise—but they quickly separated into football-watching men and chattering women. Roxie stayed with the men.

Since they had eaten throughout the day, no one was hungry when supper time came around. Marian and Roxie went home, but Francis decided to stay for the rest of the Rose Bowl.

"I hate all these *bowls!*" Roxie grumbled. "You'd think one bowl would be enough."

"Oh, there's never enough football for the men," her mother said. "We women are gentler, we don't like to see all that violence, do we?"

Roxie shrugged. "Ellie loves it. Back home she used to watch it a lot. Her mom liked it, too . . ."

Marian put her hand on Roxie's shoulder. "You always say that, Rox. 'Back home.' We're home now, dear." Roxie looked up at her. "We are, dear. This *is* our home."

XIV

Dr. Mann looked over the class and smiled brightly.

"I trust that the holidays provided you all with a time of peace and love, a time of spiritual growth together as a family and that you gave the Lord the privilege of gaining delight from your life!"

Roxie looked at Lee-Ann, who smiled, and at Bess, who didn't.

"Let's continue our study of Proverbs, chapter ten, verse twenty-nine. Bess Preger, will you read, please?"

Bess stood. " 'The way of the Lord is strength to the upright: but destruction shall be to the workers of iniquity. The righteous shall never be removed: but the wicked shall not inhabit the earth.' "

"Thank you, Bess. 'The righteous shall never be removed: but the wicked shall not inhabit the earth,' " Dr. Mann repeated. "Think about that, people. The only social security is *God's* security."

Roxie felt a tap on her forearm. Earl Clare, a boy in her Bible class whom she'd barely noticed, was pushing a folded paper toward her. She frowned at Earl and then at the paper.

"Take it," he whispered. "It's for you."

"Earl, will you please read?" Dr. Mann said as Earl coughed and fumbled with pages.

Roxie held her breath, but evidently Dr. Mann hadn't seen the note that Earl had passed to her. While Earl stammered his verse, Roxie unfolded the paper with one hand, keeping her place in her Bible with the other. The note was from Jarrell.

Please, she read. *I have to talk to you. I'll be behind the bush, you know where, right after this period. Please, Roxie. Be there.*

She looked up, but only Lee-Ann was watching her.

"Thank God you came," Jarrell said, pulling her toward him.

"What's the matter?" she asked. "Why didn't you wait till after school?"

"I wanted to make sure I'd get to *see* you after school. You hardly looked at me all day. I didn't even see you yesterday in church . . ." He glanced over his shoulder to see if anyone was watching. "What I want to do is explain to you about New Year's Eve. And I need to know how your parents feel. Just tell me now, are you mad?"

Roxie had never seen Jarrell this way. She thought he looked like a little boy, standing there, pleading with her to forgive him. She wanted to hug him.

"I'm not mad," she mumbled. "Really. I'm not."

"Come with me later. Okay?"

"Where?"

"Just away from here. Where we can talk. Come on, we've got to get in there for next period. Will you?"

"Well—I—I kind of promised my mother I'd go to the hospital with her to witness to this patient she's been seeing there—"

She hadn't promised Marian, but she was suddenly a little afraid of Jarrell and still angry with him for spoiling things at the Pregers' party.

"Call her, call your mother," Jarrell insisted. "Need change?"

"N-no, I have it," Roxie answered.

"Roxie, we have to go. Will you meet me later?"

"Yes . . ."

He nodded, touched her hand, and was gone.

Roxie watched him run toward the door and frowned. She thought about Bess, who was barely speaking to her. Roxie felt it was only a matter of time before Bess's mother talked Marian even further away from any kindness she might still feel toward Jarrell . . .

Roxie took a deep breath. She decided she would meet Jarrell, but since he wanted to apologize for New Year's she figured Kenny would probably want to apologize to Lee-Ann, too. Roxie wanted Lee-Ann with her. If Lee-Ann were there, we could handle it together, she thought. And that would be easier since she was so uncertain about Jarrell at the moment. She started for the school, thinking of where she could catch up with Lee-Ann.

*

"No, I'm not coming, Roxie."

"Oh, but Lee-Ann, Kenny will want to talk to you, too. Please come with me? It's only a quick meeting after school . . ."

"Listen, Roxie," Lee-Ann said seriously, "I've got to tell you something. The Lord does work in strange ways. I think New Year's Eve was the way He picked to show me I shouldn't hang around with Kenny any more. Or Jarrell. They are wild, Roxie. Sure, we had fun, but the Lord was warning me that that's enough. I've told lies, Roxie. Did you hear that passage we worked on today in class? 'The mouth of the just bringeth forth wisdom: but the froward tongue shall be cut out.' "

"Oh, Lee-Ann—"

"I mean it, Roxie. You should learn from it, too. I'm not seeing Kenny St. Pierre any more!"

As soon as he saw her, Jarrell grabbed her hand.

"Come on," he said, pulling her.

"Where?" she asked, beginning to hang back.

"Just come, Roxie, *please*. Come on . . ."

They walked together down the steep hill, Roxie lagging a step behind, Jarrell tugging at her hand.

"Where are we going?"

"You'll see . . . Here!" He stopped in front of a dilapidated Buick.

"This is Bill Wooster's car," Roxie said.

"Yeah, I borrowed it. Get in, okay?" He opened the passenger door for her.

"No, Jarrell, you didn't say anything about a car . . ."

He made an exasperated sound. "I got the car 'specially for this, Roxie. So we can really be private. Get in." She looked at him. *"Please* get in."

In minutes, they were out on the highway.

"I'm a good driver, Roxie. Don't worry."

"Where are we going?" she asked again.

"I thought it would be nice to drive out to the lake. It's such a warm day for this time of year . . . Some years we have that—you know, summerlike. Shirtsleeves at Christmas time . . ."

Roxie looked out the window. They had passed the residential section.

"You ever been out to Lake Winonga?" Jarrell asked.

Roxie shook her head.

"Well, it's beautiful any time of year. The color of the mountains is real pretty reflected in the water an' all. And there're only summer houses, so no people . . . Just water and woods . . . Maybe some deer . . ."

Roxie kept her eyes on the windshield. I shouldn't be here, she thought.

A stone flew up and struck the windshield on Roxie's side. Instinctively, she winced and drew back. A screen, she thought. A windscreen, a radar screen, God's radar, I'm on God's radar . . .

"Let's go back, Jarrell," she said.

"Not yet. Listen, first. I did it for Kenny. The beer, I mean. He said he just couldn't face all those stuck-up noses without getting some kind of buzz on, so that's what we really stopped at the 7-Eleven for. Kenny has a phony ID—no, Roxie, don't look away. I know it was stupid to get drunk, but I knew how Kenny felt. That whole group—your parents, Louise Hawley and her parents, Bess Preger—I know what she always thought about me. The only one in that bunch besides you and Lee-Ann who ever said 'Jarrell Meek is a nice guy' is Hope, even though she never did a thing in her life her parents and the Bible didn't say was okay." He stopped talking and stared straight ahead at the road. Roxie turned to look at his profile. "I guess you know I really care for you, Roxie," he said finally. "You're the first girl I ever told that to. I know what I did was stupid, but are you going to let it ruin everything?"

Roxie leaned forward and touched his hand. He grabbed hers and squeezed it, pulling her closer to him on the seat. They rode that way together until they reached the lake.

The water shone in the afternoon sunlight when they arrived, a slight wind making ripples and little whitecaps on the surface.

"It's beautiful," Roxie said softly, "just beautiful."

"Uh-huh," Jarrell said proudly, as if it were all his. "I told you. The water's low that way because they drop it. After the season, so they can work on their piers . . . the folks who have summer places here . . ."

"What are those big piles of branches for?" Roxie asked, pointing toward the shoreline.

"Those? Oh, those are old crappie beds."

"*What* beds?" Roxie giggled.

"Crappies. They're like little sunfish. Folks bring their

Christmas trees, branches, sticks, all that stuff, and they make beds for the crappies to spawn in and then they can catch 'em easy."

"Now?"

"No, not now. In the spring. You really like it here?"

"Yes," Roxie breathed.

"That's what I thought. That's why I wanted to bring you. Look around. All you can see are mountains and trees—pine and hickory nut, water oaks—the pines keep it all green, but this time of year, the leaves from the other trees make a floor about four inches thick. Feel it? It's just like a carpet . . ."

Roxie gave a tiny gasp.

"You see a deer?" Jarrell asked.

"No. It wasn't a deer. It was a person!"

"What?"

"It was someone running. I thought it was a deer at first because I wasn't expecting to see a person, but it was, Jarrell, it was." She huddled closer to him.

"Well, don't be afraid. It was probably one of the summer folks out here working on his beds early or something."

"No, it wasn't like that. The person was running. Like he didn't want us to see him. Jarrell?"

"What?"

"I don't think he had any clothes on. Or she. Maybe it was a she. I couldn't tell, it was so quick!"

"I'll go look," Jarrell said. "Where? That cluster of pines over there?"

He had tennis shoes on and though he tried to tiptoe, it was hard to be quiet with leaves crunching underfoot. In a moment, he had disappeared into the thicket where

Roxie had pointed. Roxie waited, chewing her thumb-nail and watching for him to reappear.

When he did, she ran toward him but he waved her back, looking over his shoulder as he walked.

"You were right," he said as he approached her. "I saw her but she didn't see me. I cracked a twig and she looked up. Probably thought I was a deer . . . Anyway, she won't be coming out to check, though, that's for sure . . ."

"*Who?*"

"Molly Seeds."

Roxie clapped a hand to her mouth.

"She was with someone. I couldn't tell who it was, probably Cornell Abney . . . She's been running around with him . . ."

"The senior?"

Jarrell nodded. "She had her top off, but not her skirt . . ."

"Molly Seeds . . ." Roxie whispered.

Jarrell was shaking his head. "I don't care what stories you've heard about Molly, Roxie, and there are plenty, *I* know. If she's wild, she's got reasons. Folks like to say Molly was born bad but saw the light. *I* say it was the light *made* her wild."

Roxie frowned at him.

"I don't mean the Lord made her bad, Roxie. What I mean is—look: my father's strict, *everybody's* father's strict . . . Mr. Hawley, Mr. St. Pierre—I guess you know. But Molly's father takes the big prize. Tommy-John Seeds . . . Whew . . ." Jarrell whistled softly.

"How? What do you mean? What's he like?" Roxie asked.

"Tommy-John Seeds is so strict with his religion, he doesn't even see his family as—as people. So while he's pushing religion into each of 'em, he's killing 'em! Roxie, he doesn't see it!"

"How do you mean, the strictness of religion—with Molly?" Roxie asked. She was thinking of the Pregers—surely they were strict about their religion, but Bess wasn't like Molly.

"Well," Jarrell answered, "he beats up on her. But badly! And for the slightest little thing she does. That's not a rumor, Roxie, I've seen it. Tommy-John doesn't care who's around sometimes . . ." He turned away from Roxie and looked off toward the lake. "Mrs. Seeds is real sick. I'm not sure with what, but I think it's mental. Thomas Junior, he's pretty dumb, but he works hard and doesn't say much. Mr. Seeds hits him, too, though, but not like he does Molly. Diane, she's little, so it's hard to say about her yet, but I'm bettin' she'll get it, too. Kenny says Mrs. Seeds is squirrelly because of a whack she got around her ears."

"He hits them because of his religion?" Roxie asked. She was suddenly reminded of her father's remark about brawling over a discussion of prayer in the schools. "What does he think? That he'll beat the fear of the Lord into them?"

Jarrell tilted his head. "Yeah," he said nodding. "Something like that. He quotes the Bible while he does the whipping. I heard him once when he was working on Molly with his belt, out behind the school. I don't know what it was he caught her doing, but what he was quoting was Proverbs." He snorted. "That much I *did* hear. And he locks her up in a closet he's got in his basement sometimes, and screams whole passages at her while she's in there. My daddy would never lock me in a closet but I've had my share of whippings . . ."

"He locks her in a closet . . ." Roxie whispered, almost to herself.

"To make her concentrate on her duty to the Lord," Jarrell said. "All he has to do is get one whisper that Molly's done something he disapproves of, which is just about anything, believe it! And he won't even feed her in there—a whole day, maybe more.

"Last spring, Molly woke up the Foulks family at four o'clock in the morning. She was just beating on their door, like to wake up the whole neighborhood. Woke *me* up. And my mama . . ."

"The Foulks family? Brainard Foulks?"

"Uh-huh. Brainard. He lives on my street, that's how I know. At first I was mad because Mama got woken up . . . My mama and daddy are older—you know—and Mama has arthritis pretty bad. So she needs her rest. I got up quick to see what was going on and there was Molly, just beating on the Foulks's door . . ."

"But why?"

"Roxie, she only wanted to be with him. Just be with him. Tommy-John just thinks of all of his family like—like they're his *things,* not like they're people. I've seen it, I've seen it, the children are *things* you're supposed to pump full of stuff and then turn 'em loose to do the same thing to *their* kids. But I know Molly Seeds . . . She just wants to be with anyone who'll show her a little affection or something that's loving. And she was yelling about how Brainard'd promised he was going to meet her and she'd waited and waited and he'd never shown up. I'd bet anything he did promise her, too, and then just forgot about it or changed his mind . . . Roxie, it was so sad. She started crying, 'Brainard, I thought you wanted to be with me, I thought you said we could be together . . .' "

"But everybody's not like that, Jarrell," Roxie said, thinking again of the Pregers, of Hope and Lee-Ann. Of her own mother. "You can be religious and still love your children . . . Still show them love . . ."

"Oh, yeah, Roxie, but—" Jarrell stopped and searched for the words he wanted. "But there are so many peo-ple—so many—where the love gets lost in the *duty*. In the *rules*. And you can't love unless the rules are fol-lowed. And it's all what God wants, they say . . . You can't love unless the rules are followed . . ." he re-peated and rubbed the back of his wrist over his mouth. "Sometimes, I swear, I have dreams about Molly cryin', 'Don't you wanna be with me?' "

Roxie shivered and wrapped her arms tightly around herself.

Jarrell cleared his throat. "Anyway, the Foulks came to the door and called Molly a slut and told her to go away. The whole neighborhood was out by that time . . . And I guess someone called Molly's father because pretty soon, up drives ol' Tommy-John Seeds in that old Ford pick-up he gets to run if he kicks it hard enough."

Roxie peered off into the woods to see if she could see anyone moving, but all was still. "What happened?" she whispered.

"Molly's father screamed at Brainard for seducing his daughter, yelled that it was all Brainard's fault. And Brainard's mama screamed about how Molly was a slut and a tramp and the whole town knew it. And pretty soon, Tommy-John was dragging Molly down the Foulks's walk by the back of her neck and he shoved her into that truck so hard she hit her head on the steering wheel. I saw it."

"Oh," Roxie breathed.

"But the thing is, Molly just hungers. Just hungers, is all. And all the Bible reading in the world doesn't fill her up . . ."

"Bible reading . . ." Roxie murmured.

They stood for a long while without saying anything more. Then Jarrell took Roxie's hand.

"Let's go sit down by the water," he said. "Just for a little while. Where it's peaceful . . ."

She followed where he led and they found a rotted log at the edge of the shoreline.

"This is a good place," Jarrell said and held her hand while she sat. "Do you forgive me for New Year's?" he asked finally.

Roxie nodded, not looking at him.

He leaned over, took her face in his hands and kissed her. It was, she thought, the nicest kiss she'd ever had.

"I'm not going to rush you into anything, Roxie, I promise you," Jarrell told her. "Whatever you say is okay with me . . ."

Roxie shivered again. She felt grateful, excited, warm. But she did no more than look at him.

"Jarrell, let's go now. I wouldn't want Molly to see us and think we were spying on her."

Without a word, he pulled her to her feet and they walked slowly back toward Bill Wooster's car.

*

Roxie wasn't sure when it began.

Bess had been standoffish and aloof ever since the New Year's Eve party. But the other girls hadn't seemed any different. Now they did.

At Youthlight meetings, they seemed less friendly. Even Hope and Lee-Ann. They began to exclude her from little projects, leaving her out of their private talks together. Even some of the boys did the same to Jarrell, though they were more overt, loudly kidding with each other during Jarrell's solos until they were hushed by the music teacher.

Roxie's little social group seemed to have dissolved around her. She mentioned it once to Hope, but Hope looked away, murmuring that it was just Roxie's imagination. Roxie was left staring at Hope's retreating back.

Dr. Arman sat at his desk with his hands folded in front of him. His lips were set in a tight line as he waited for a response from Lucas Meek, sitting across from him in a leather chair, with his cap in his hands. But Lucas Meek only stared back at the school principal, his Adam's apple bobbing as he kept swallowing.

"You did hear me, Mr. Meek?" the principal asked.

"I ain't deaf," Lucas Meek mumbled. He took his eyes from Dr. Arman's face and looked instead at a calendar on the wall next to him. Printed on it was a big, bold 13, with THURSDAY, JAN. under it in black letters. Lucky thirteen, he thought. "You better be wrong, though," he said finally.

"Well, there was a witness," Dr. Arman said, clearing his throat. "I'm not at liberty to name the individual, yet. But this person claims that it was your son, along with Kenneth St. Pierre, by the way, and some other people whom the witness didn't recognize, who were responsible for the destruction of the church's antenna on New Year's Eve. Now, you know nothing of this?"

"Nothing, I swear."

"Of course, we're going to have to suspend your son and Kenneth St. Pierre until we've investigated the charge . . ."

"I'll break his neck," Lucas Meek mumbled under his breath.

"Beg your pardon?"

"I was just thinking how it takes all my savings to send Jarrell to this school, give him a good Christian education, make him a credit to the Lord . . . My daughter even helps us out with the tuition and it's hard for her and her husband . . ."

"I'm very sorry, Mr. Meek," the principal said, his hands still folded. "But it's a serious charge and we must follow up on it. I'm going to have to call Jarrell down here to the office but I wanted to talk with you, first. I'm sorry to have to take you away from work."

Lucas Meek inhaled loudly.

"I assume," the principal continued, "that you'd like to be here when I talk with Jarrell?"

"Oh, yeah. I'll be here, all right . . ."

Dr. Arman's announcement came over the loudspeaker during the lunch period.

"Will Jarrell Meek please report to the office? Jarrell Meek. To the office, please."

There was silence in the lunchroom as Jarrell stood and carried his tray toward the trash basket. The other students looked at Jarrell, looked at Roxie, looked away. The silence hung over the room even after Jarrell had left, and before the usual hum of voices could begin again, there was a second announcement:

"Will Kenneth St. Pierre report to the office, please? Kenneth St. Pierre."

Again, all eyes were on Kenny as he, too, walked with his tray toward the front of the room. And again, they looked at Roxie, whose face was almost scarlet, as she sat at a corner table near the back of the cafeteria.

Roxie knew her face was hot, hated that she had no control over it. She forced herself to bite into her sandwich, which had the taste of dry sand. They all know something, she thought. They all know and I'm the only one who doesn't.

Jarrell did not return to class that afternoon. He was not at the Youthlight meeting, which Roxie made herself attend, and he did not visit the children at the hospital that night. Roxie tried to call him and got his mother—twice—who said that Jarrell was very busy and could not come to the phone. She called Kenny and got no answer at all.

Bess was the one who told her. And only when Roxie had swallowed her pride and confronted Bess outside her house the next morning.

"I'm surprised you didn't hear," Bess said in a flat voice. "Dr. Caraman found out it was Jarrell and Kenny who were responsible for wrecking the antenna New Year's Eve."

"*What?*" Roxie fairly screamed. "That's crazy! How could two boys do something like that?"

"They weren't alone," Bess said in that same flat voice. "There were other people with them. They're trying to get Jarrell and Kenny to tell who they were. Probably people who were drunk, just like they were."

"I don't believe you!" Roxie cried.

"Don't then. That's why they were called to the office yesterday. Everybody knows."

Roxie went to school. She sat through all her classes without hearing a word of what was being said. At three o'clock she went right by the waiting bus and walked home by herself. She spent the afternoon in her room, on her bed. It wasn't until she heard Marian calling her for supper that she realized she had fallen asleep.

"What is it, Roxie, you're not eating," her mother said, halfway through the meal.

"Nothing."

"Come on, now, dear. You haven't said a word, you haven't even lifted your fork—"

Something inside Roxie exploded. "Nothing!" she shrieked. She jumped up from the table, knocking over her chair, and the shocked expressions on her parents' faces didn't even register in her mind as she bolted from the room.

*

She heard the knock on her door five minutes later. Is that Mom or Daddy? she thought. Mom. No, Daddy. She almost giggled, but there were tears, instead. She let them seep into the pillow, making no attempt to reach for the tissue box on her night table.

"Rox?" A frightened voice through the door.

Daddy, Roxie thought. Good . . .

"Okay to come in?" Francis asked, and when she didn't answer, he pushed the door open slightly. "Roxie?" he said softly.

She turned her face away, but he came into the room anyway and sat down on the edge of her bed.

"I never saw you like this, Rox," he said, touching her back. She began to sob loudly at his touch.

"Come on," Francis said, stroking her shoulder. "Let's have it. All of it, right now . . ."

"They acc-accused Jarrell and K-Kenny of knocking down the tower," she stammered through her sobs, "and no one will t-talk to me and Jarrell will probably be expelled and Kenny, too, and no one in the whole school likes me any more . . ."

Francis closed his eyes. It always made him feel helpless when the women in his family cried.

"Honey, what does the tower business have to do with you? I don't really understand. *Was* Jarrell responsible?"

"I don't know. I don't think so. I can't believe he was, and anyway, he would have told me . . ."

"What does it have to do with you?" Francis repeated. "I can't believe people would be mean to you, just because you've gone out with Jarrell—"

"I don't know, I don't know," she cried. Francis handed her a tissue and she blew her nose loudly, feeling eight years old. "They must think I'm contaminated or something. But they won't sit with me or talk to me . . ." She slapped at her pillow. "It's not that they're mean or anything, they just—oh, I don't know—" She rolled over and cried until she couldn't cry any more, and Francis held her shaking shoulders until she stopped. After a while, thinking she was asleep, he tiptoed out. But Roxie wasn't sleeping.

Downstairs, Marian was waiting.

"What is it?" she asked anxiously.

"Did you know they accused Jarrell of having something to do with Caraman's antenna being knocked down?" Francis said, as he descended the stairs.

"No!"

"Shh—" He looked up toward Roxie's door. "Let's go into the kitchen . . ."

Marian rushed after him. "Did he do it? *Jarrell?*"

"Roxie doesn't think so. And the other kids haven't been very friendly toward her, so she's doubly upset."

"Well, Roxie didn't have anything to do with it!"

"No, of course not. I don't know what it is, maybe guilt by association or something. Roxie used the word *contaminated* . . ."

"Well, I knew the Pregers were upset by the boys' behavior at their New Year's Eve party. We all were. What do you think, Frank?"

"I think I'm upset that my daughter is so unhappy," he said.

Marian was frowning. "But do you think that—you know—'where there's smoke . . .'?"

"What?"

"Well, the boy *had* been drinking that night. He was

more or less forced to leave the party. And Cynthia's hinted that he may not be the best influence on Roxie, although he's always behaved well, except for that one time . . ."

"Marian, please don't make judgments until the whole story comes out. Especially around Roxie. I think she's sleeping now . . ."

The phone rang at eleven o'clock. Francis answered. It was Jarrell, for Roxie. The call lasted less than thirty seconds.

Both Roxie's parents made no pretense of not listening. Each stood on one side of her as she held the phone, although most of the conversation on Roxie's end consisted of monosyllables. "Yes—" she said, and "What—" and "I do—" and "Okay, bye."

She hung up and looked into her parents' anxious faces.

"He said he didn't do it. He promised it. But he said he couldn't go back to school yet and that I should trust him and that he loved me and he'd try to see me soon but he didn't know when." She began to cry again. "Mom?" she said. "Dad? Can I go visit Glenna? Can I go away for just a while? Please can I visit Glenna, Daddy?"

"Roxie," Marian said, "now, listen to me. I don't think this is the time for you to leave. If you do that, everyone will think you had something to do with what happened. You've been associated with the Meek boy and I think you should go to school the way you've always done and hold your head up. Because you had nothing to do with that criminal act. It's bad enough you're linked so closely with the boy."

"Marian—" Francis began, but Roxie interrupted.

"He said he didn't do it, Mother!"

"If that's true, then the Lord will point that out. But until He does, people are going to believe what they believe and I don't want anyone thinking that you are involved!"

Francis moved toward Roxie and put his arm around her shoulder.

"Honey, it'll work out," he said. "Either your friend's in trouble or he's not, but we've got to take it one step at a time till it's all settled. Come on now—" He squeezed her shoulder. "You'll get through this all right, trying as it is . . ."

Roxie buried her face against his chest.

"Roxie—" Marian said, "I'll pray for Jarrell . . ."

XV

Roxie went to school with her heart pounding. Each day she had been hopeful of a kind word or gesture from one of the girls and each day they seemed to draw farther and farther away. When Lee-Ann walked past her in the corridor without even turning her head, something snapped inside Roxie. She reached out and grabbed Lee-Ann's arm. Startled, Lee-Ann only looked at her with wide eyes.

"Aren't you speaking to me at all, Lee-Ann?" Roxie asked. She hadn't meant to sound cold, but to her ears she sounded so. She went on hurriedly. "—Because I have to speak to you. I want you to know that Jarrell and Kenny are innocent, they really didn't do it, Lee-Ann. I talked to Jarrell last night and he told me—"

But Lee-Ann interrupted her. "Roxie," she said, shaking her head, "you don't understand. Remember we talked about punishment that night when we first double-dated? Remember Psalms: 'Blessed is the man that walketh not in the counsel of the ungodly . . .'? Both of us—we strayed, you know we did. But we can come back. *I* have. Pray for Jarrell and Kenny, Roxie, but don't follow them any more. Don't follow, don't go with them. I just won't put my feet on that path any more, Roxie, I've already told you that." She began to walk away but Roxie wouldn't let her leave.

"No, *you* don't understand, Lee-Ann," she said. "Look, it's lunch, you have time, just talk to me for a minute."

Lee-Ann stopped, sighed, leaned against the wall. "I don't know what else I can say, Roxie," she said.

"You can say that you believe in Kenny. And Jarrell. You know them. You know they wouldn't do what they're accused of and they need friends, Lee-Ann." She stopped herself from adding, so do I.

"Well, it's awful hard not to believe they did it," Lee-Ann said, "because they were seen by someone."

"What?"

"They were seen. There was a witness. I guess you didn't hear."

Roxie put her hand against the wall to steady herself. She felt suddenly weak. "Who?" she asked in a small voice.

"Oh, Roxie, it doesn't matter—"

"Of course it matters!" Roxie's dizziness vanished as quickly as it had come. "Who was it?" she asked again.

"I don't think I should tell you," Lee-Ann said. "Not because I want to keep secrets, Roxie, but because I think it would probably do more harm than good. You need to concentrate on your prayers, on planting your feet back on the path of righteousness, not on individual—"

"You better tell me, Lee-Ann," Roxie said in a low

voice. "I'll find out anyway, you know I will, so you just better tell me who the witness was."

Lee-Ann looked at Roxie's face. She clicked her tongue against her teeth.

"All right," she said resignedly. "I guess you will find out if you really want to so I'll tell you. But, Roxie, try not to let it get in the way of what you must do—" She sighed. "It was Louise Hawley. She was out walking. You know, after she left the party. There were people on the streets, she wanted to get away by herself, so she headed out toward the fields—"

"Louise—Hawley—" Roxie whispered.

"—at the edge of town, toward the hill where the tower stood. And she heard laughter and noise even out there and it bothered and scared her, so she hid and she saw them."

Roxie closed her eyes. "But it was dark, Lee-Ann. How could she see just who it was, if she saw anything at all!"

"She could tell. She recognized the voices and the shapes, she said. She saw them and there were some others, too. Big men. Or boys. But big. There'd have to have been others, because they'd've needed help with something that large—"

"But Jarrell and Kenny left the party long after Louise did," Roxie said. "It couldn't have been them!"

"No," Lee-Ann said, "it wasn't that long after. And Louise walked around for a while before she went out to the fields. They had lots of time to get there. Louise said she's been wrestling with her conscience all these days since New Year's, but she just had to come out and tell." Lee-Ann ignored the face Roxie made. "Anyway, Louise was real scared. She just ran right home afterward. She was in bed, shaking like a leaf, when her parents got there."

"I can't believe you and everyone else would take Louise Hawley's word for something like this," Roxie said angrily. "Everyone knows how she feels about Jarrell! Everyone knows that!"

"But she saw it," Lee-Ann said firmly. "She was a witness."

"That's only what she *says,* Lee-Ann!" Roxie cried and quickly put her fingers to her lips. People walking by turned to look at her and she turned her face away, toward the wall.

Lee-Ann leaned close to her. "Listen to me, Roxie," Lee-Ann said, "you must pray. Keep in your mind that this is all in God's hands. It is not for *you* to do anything. Remember that or you'll never have peace. This is a testing, Roxie, we have them all our lives."

"There must be something we can do," Roxie whispered, her forehead still pressed against the cold tile wall. "We can talk to Louise. She can't be telling the truth. You know how she is. At least we can do that—talk to her . . ."

"We can't call Louise a liar," Lee-Ann said. "We can't say she lied, Roxie."

"But we can ask her, can't we? We don't have to accuse her, but maybe if we talked to her, she'd say something, change her story, *something!* Don't you care about Kenny at all? Wouldn't you want to help him if you could?"

"Oh, Roxie, you're not listening to me, you're not

listening to what God wants. I *am* helping Kenny. I'm *praying* for him. Don't you see that if Jarrell and Kenny really are innocent then they'll come out of this just fine? Don't you see that, Roxie? There isn't anything that you or I or any human being can do but trust in the Lord. Let the Lord do His job, Roxie. Don't you try to do it for Him!"

Roxie was shivering as Lee-Ann walked away down the hall.

I have to do it myself, she thought. I have to talk to Louise or I'll just go crazy!

But Louise managed to slip away each time she saw a determined-looking Roxie approaching—in the corridor outside of class, in the girls' room, at the back of the prayer chapel. It was at the very end of physical education that Roxie was able to get close enough to speak to her.

"Hi, Roxie, I'm in kind of a hurry," Louise said all in one breath as she moved toward the door.

"This won't take long, Louise," Roxie said. "It's about Jarrell." As if you didn't know, she thought.

"What about Jarrell?" Louise asked.

"I know all about it, Louise, so you don't have to pretend. I don't think you could have any idea of what could happen to Jarrell and Kenny. This isn't just some kind of prank you accused them of, it's a criminal offense."

Louise stiffened. "I saw what I saw," she said. "*I* wasn't drunk that night." She moved away, but Roxie grabbed her arm.

"Did you *really* see them, Louise? Were you there? We all know how angry you were at them that night. And even if you did go all the way out to the field, are you sure it was Jarrell you saw or Jarrell you *wanted* to see?"

Pulling her arm away, Louise glared at Roxie. "You have no right to talk to me that way, Roxie Cable. We're on our honor here. It's bad enough it took me so long to get up my courage to tell. My conscience is clear. And I'm glad you found out and turned from Satan in time. You should be grateful to me!"

I *am* going crazy, Roxie thought. I am, I know it—

She sat in her Bible studies class, hardly hearing Dr. Mann. She looked at Bess's earnest profile as the girl mouthed the words Dr. Mann was reviewing for the class.

" 'Discretion shall preserve thee, understanding shall keep thee . . .' "

Roxie shuddered. She couldn't swallow.

" 'To deliver thee from the way of the evil man, from the man that speaketh froward things; . . .' "

Roxie coughed once, then found she couldn't stop. Someone patted her on the back, but there were tears in her eyes and on her cheeks.

" 'Who leave the paths of uprightness to walk in the ways of darkness' . . ."

"No . . ." Roxie moaned softly. She hadn't realized she'd spoken aloud. When Bess and the others turned in their seats to look at her, she covered her face with her hands and sobbed loudly, mortified and miserable.

Bess looked at Dr. Mann, who nodded, and she was on her feet at once, beckoning to Lee-Ann to follow. With their arms around Roxie, they led her from the classroom to the teachers' lounge across the hall, where they put her on a couch. Lee-Ann smoothed her hair back from her forehead, while Bess kept a firm hand on her shoulder.

"It's all right, now," Bess whispered soothingly. "You've heard the voice of the Lord, Roxie, you'll be all right now . . ." She smiled at Lee-Ann over Roxie's heaving shoulders.

That night, the Cables' doorbell rang. Francis opened it to find Bess Preger looking up at him.

"Is Roxie here?"

Francis peered at her. At any other time he would have laughed. Her tone was exactly like one he'd always heard at wakes and funerals. But instead, he merely smiled at Bess and stepped aside to let her in.

"Rox?" he called up the stairs. "It's Bess!"

"May I just go right up, Mr. Cable?" Bess asked.

Francis frowned. "What's going on, Bess? Is Roxie okay? She hardly ate anything at dinner. Everything all right between you girls now?"

"Everything will be all right now, Mr. Cable," Bess said. "And Roxie's fine, she really is. I just know it. I'm going up now, to see her." Before he could say more, she was halfway up the stairs.

She tapped softly at Roxie's door.

"Come in, Bess . . ."

"Hi," Bess said, her hand on the doorknob.

Roxie looked up at her. "Thank you for . . . what you did for me this afternoon," she said. "I thought I was on your hate list or something . . ."

Bess pulled up Roxie's desk chair and sat down.

"Oh, no, honey," she said. "I'm sorry you thought that. It's just that I, myself, and the other girls—well, we've been taught always to avoid anything, just anything, that identifies with the counterculture. Anything that's in direct opposition to the Christian life. I was so afraid for you, Roxie, but when Dr. Mann was reading Proverbs today and I saw your face and you broke down that way . . . Well, I knew that Jesus was truly back in your heart . . ."

Roxie didn't say anything, so Bess continued quickly.

"Jarrell Meek—he's always walked on the edge. Well, you've seen for yourself. Why, you've seen more than I have, so you know what he's like."

"The point is, I do know what he's like," Roxie said. "Maybe he doesn't conform to everything you want him to, but he's really a good person. Kind."

Bess took a breath. "I know how confused you must still be, Roxie. That's why I'm here. You see, we're all sinners. And temptation is always beckoning, always. But we must be strong. We mustn't give in to the Devil's voice. Jarrell and Kenny St. Pierre—why, they just give in all the time. Jarrell'd be the first to tell you, I've known him since we were small!

"Roxie, now listen to me: Do you know why we're here? Why we're on earth?"

Roxie frowned at Bess.

" 'Thou art worthy, O Lord, to receive glory and

honor and power: for Thou hast created all things, and for Thy pleasure they are and were created.' Revelation, chapter four, verse eleven. We were created for God's pleasure, Roxie, don't you see? That's our purpose, our reason for being. So don't you see how wrong it is to live just for our own selfish pleasure? Don't you see that just pleasing yourself and your little world isn't enough? You belong to God, Roxie, by right of creation, not to yourself. When you go along with the bad things that Jarrell Meek does, it's just like going along with the Devil himself. It is, Roxie, if you just think about it, you'll see. If you're a true believer, you can have full assurance of salvation and be eternally secure in Christ, who never leaves you."

Roxie bit her lower lip and looked helplessly about the room. Bess took her hand and went on speaking in a firm voice.

"I have been praying so hard for you, Roxie, for your happiness and peace, praying to keep you from having to spend eternity in Hell. Please ask Christ to forgive you, please, Roxie. Jarrell will, too. Believe me, he will. I know his father."

Roxie pulled her hand away. "Bess—I didn't have anything to do with the antenna—"

"Oh, I know that, I do! Why, Roxie, you were right there at my house—"

"And Jarrell didn't either! He told me!"

Bess sighed. "You don't really know Jarrell, Roxie," she said.

"I know him better than you—"

"You don't. Really. I know Jarrell only too well. My brother was just like him!"

Roxie shivered, exactly as she had when Bess had first mentioned her older brother. It seemed light-years ago, though Roxie knew at that moment that Joseph Junior had always been there, concealed somewhere in a corner of her mind, coloring all the different emotions she'd felt toward Bess from the beginning.

"Please listen, Roxie," Bess said desperately. " 'The righteousness of the perfect shall direct his way: but the wicked shall fall by his own wickedness.' 'He that diligently seeketh good procureth favor: but he that seeketh mischief, it shall come unto him.' "

"Bess, this isn't the time to quote at me!"

"It's *always* the time, that's what I'm trying to tell you! Listen to the Lord's plan!" Bess cried. "Roxie, it's you I'm concerned with! You've been sorely tested, but our loving Lord works in mysterious ways and the Devil that's been tempting you has thankfully been called to account. You're most surely back on the path of obedience and submission, Roxie, you realize that the only security lies in Christ and it's happened before anything went too far. Roxie, don't you see how the Lord stepped in and saved you?"

"Oh, Bess, but—but Jarrell—"

"Roxie, do you believe I'm your friend? Do you? Do you believe I want only your happiness and your peace and your eternal salvation?"

"Yes . . ." It was almost a whimper.

"Then pray with me. That's the real reason I'm here. To pray with you. Kneel down, Roxie." She moved from the chair and knelt at the side of Roxie's bed. "Please!" she implored.

Roxie knelt. Bess smiled gratefully at her.

Roxie prayed that Louise Hawley might fall by her own wickedness.

There was a rap on Roxie's door. She opened her eyes, wondering how long she and Bess had been kneeling next to one another.

"Roxie? Bess?" Marian called.

Roxie stood, calling, "It's all right—you can come in, Mom . . ."

Bess moved to a sitting position on the floor.

"Well, Bess, dear," Marian said, stepping into the room. "Your mother just called. It's getting so late."

"I'm sorry, Mrs. Cable," Bess said, rising. "I just didn't realize. We were talking, Roxie and I, and the time just went so fast—"

But Marian held up her hand. "Now, don't worry," she said. "Your mother's not angry. She'd just expected you earlier, that's all, and she wanted to make sure everything was all right. I told her it was, right?"

"Yes, ma'am," Bess said and smiled.

"And your mother said for you to be sure and finish whatever it was you wanted to say to Roxie because she knew how important it was. I just wanted you to know she called, that's all, honey."

"Thank you, Mrs. Cable, but we're about finished now," Bess said. "Aren't we, Roxie?"

Roxie fell into bed as soon as Bess had left, and sleep came, but only briefly. She had longed for the escape of sleep but found herself wide awake for most of the night. Occasionally she dozed. And dreamed. In a vaporous haze she saw Bess in a long pale blue gown, with her arms and her head raised toward heaven and Roxie groaned in her sleep when the dream-Bess turned around to show the large angel wings flowing from her back.

In one of the dreams she saw Jarrell, his mouth forming an agonized O, with flames shooting up from his feet and from behind his back. That was when her cry brought Francis, rushing to her room to stroke her forehead and wait until he thought she slept again.

Finally, it was to Glenna that Roxie poured out her misery. In a six-page, tear-stained letter, she wrote all of the events and feelings she could remember—New Year's, the lake, Jarrell and Kenny, the behavior of the girls at school, the confrontation with Louise Hawley, the sudden, overwhelming feeling of pressure and confusion that caused her to break down in class, Bess's visit and, finally, even her horrible dreams. She was crying again by the time she finished the letter but she felt somewhat better. Just putting it all down on paper seemed to help. She took the letter to the post office the moment she finished, hoping it would reach her sister that much faster than if she'd put it in the mailbox on the corner of her street.

"Poor Louise," Hope said, as the girls walked to the bus after school. "She feels so awful. Look at her over there."

Louise was walking alone in the other direction, hugging her books to her chest and hunching over them.

"She'll feel better when it's all over. And she's taking comfort from the Lord, we know that," Bess said, and turned to Roxie. "I'm so happy for you," she said. "You're in harmony with God's plan again. 'To him that overcometh will I grant to sit with me in my throne even as I also overcame, and am set down with my Father in his throne.' Revelation, three." Bess put her arms through Roxie's and Lee-Ann's.

"I do feel glad again, Roxie, don't you? 'Finally, my brethren, be strong in the Lord and in the power of His might. Put on the whole armor of God, that ye may be able to stand against the wiles of the Devil.' "

Roxie looked at the two girls on either side of her.

Hope, who had been a few steps ahead, turned back with a smile. "Don't you feel the peace, Roxie?" she asked. "And the joy? The Lord's taken over. It's out of your hands."

Jarrell managed to call her again when both his parents were out—a rare occasion, since one of them was assigned to guard duty, as he called it, all the time.

"My mother—she's so hurt, Roxie," he said.

Roxie's voice caught. She couldn't say anything.

"I love you, Roxie," he said. "I didn't do anything wrong. There's going to be a police investigation, did you know that? It won't be just our word against Louise Hawley's. I had a feeling it was Louise all along . . ."

Roxie leaned against the wall and closed her eyes. It's out of my hands, she thought. If he isn't guilty he'll be all right . . . Bess says . . . Everyone believes that, everyone . . . She rubbed her temple with her fingers.

"I want to see you, Roxie," Jarrell said. "It's the only thing I think about. I'll find a way, I promise. I'll call and let you know when, okay?"

"Yes," Roxie answered. "Yes, Jarrell. I wish I could see you, too . . ."

"Roxie?"

"What, Mom?"

Marian only looked at her. She had taken to doing this often—calling Roxie's name, but not saying anything—just studying her daughter's face.

"What is it, Mom?" Roxie repeated.

"It's nothing. I don't have anything to say." She gave a little laugh. "I just like knowing you're here, we're together, we're a family . . . We're all right."

"I understand," Roxie said.

"I know you do," her mother said.

It was a Wednesday evening in late January.

Roxie was passing by the hall phone and so was able to pick it up after one ring.

"Oh, Roxie, I'm glad it's you. I have to whisper . . . Can you hear me?"

"Jarrell?"

"Listen, I have to be quick. My father's out at my sister's place and my mother won't leave me—but she needs me to go to the store for her medication. She's real bad or she'd go herself and make me go along." He chuckled. "My father would kill her if she didn't . . ." He suddenly clamped his palm over the receiver and Roxie heard a muffled sound. "No, it's okay. She's upstairs. Look, I'm finally getting to leave the house alone. I can't believe it. Meet me . . . on the corner of Van Lott Avenue, near the Piggly Wiggly. You know where?"

Roxie clutched the phone to her ear with both hands. She was shivering.

"I know it's prayer meeting night—" Jarrell continued. Roxie had forgotten. "But you can still go, you'll just be a little late, is all. You can do that, can't you?"

"I—I . . ." Roxie stammered.

Jarrell took a quick breath. "I have to go," he said. "Be there for me in fifteen minutes, okay? Okay, Roxie?" He hung up.

Roxie continued to grip the phone. She realized she'd barely spoken at all.

"Francis?" she heard her mother call. "Frank? We'll be late! Come on down!" Marian stepped into the hall. "Oh, Roxie, dear. Are you ready? Who was on the phone?"

Roxie felt dizzy. "Uh, nothing important . . ." she answered, putting the receiver back in its cradle. "Nothing, really . . ."

"Well, are you all set to go? Get your heavy jacket, honey, it's chillier tonight . . ."

"Mom . . ." Roxie opened the closet door. "I might be just a little late for prayer meeting. I have an errand to run. And then I'll get over there . . ."

"Well, how? I mean, if we leave now—"

"Don't worry, I'll be there," Roxie answered impatiently.

"Well—" Marian said hesitantly, "not too late, I hope

. . ." She fluffed Roxie's hair as a quick pacifying gesture. "You're sure you won't have any trouble getting there?"

"I'm sure, Mom . . . I won't be long."

As Marian climbed the stairs to see what was keeping Francis, Roxie opened the front door. It was six-forty-five and dark out. She pulled on her jacket.

It will be all right, she told herself. It will have to be. Just this once—it's been so long since I've seen him . . . And he's counting on me . . .

She zipped her jacket and stepped outside. I won't be too late for church, she thought. She'd walked before. This time she'd run and make better time.

"Roxie!" a voice called.

She whirled. The Pregers' car had backed down their driveway and Bess was calling to her from an open window.

"Why don't we all go together?" Bess cried. "Your parents, too! Hope's here—she had dinner with us—but we can all fit if you don't mind sitting on one of our laps!"

Roxie stared at the car.

"Go ask your mama, Roxie, we'll wait! Oh, just a minute—" Bess pulled her head back into the car for a word with someone, then leaned out again. "Roxie? Hope says we should all go over to her house afterward, okay? She's got some new clothes she had the nerve to buy without us!"

Roxie knew she wasn't focusing. Bess's face, under the street light, began to waver. The sound of Bess's voice blurred into Jarrell's.

Look, I'm finally getting to leave the house . . .

—Bess's happy, expectant face—

. . . *Leave the house alone . . . Meet me! . . .*

"Roxie?"

Roxie felt herself breathing faster. Everyone was pulling at her, calling at her, screaming. Everyone wanted something from her. Everyone was waiting!

What if Jarrell could prove his innocence? What if he couldn't? What if the investigation somehow showed he did it, even if he didn't? What if he did? What if . . .

He's waiting.

. . . *on the corner of Van Lott Avenue . . . You can do that, can't you?*

"Roxie, hey there!"

Oh, Bess, Roxie thought. Bess, with nothing better to think about but prayer meeting and Hope's new clothes!

Meet me . . .

Roxie closed her eyes tightly. She longed for Glenna. She wanted her sister!

Cynthia Preger opened her car door and stepped out.

"Roxie, are you all right, honey?" she called. "Did you hear Bess? We'll all go together if you'll just call your mama and daddy!"

"Mrs. P—Preger . . ." was all Roxie could manage. She peered up the street, though she knew Van Lott Avenue wasn't visible from her porch steps. He's alone out there, she thought. There's no one on his side . . . She felt trapped for Jarrell, for herself . . .

"Yes, honey, it's me!" Cynthia yelled back. "Now come on, we're waiting for y'all!"

The door opened behind Roxie and her parents crossed the porch toward her.

"Why, there you are, you slowpokes," Cynthia said, resting her elbow on the car roof. "Hop in now, or we'll be late!"

"Well, Cynthia, how nice," Marian said. "Isn't it, Frank? Now we can all go together. Roxie, here you are! I'm so relieved you changed your mind about that errand, it's so dark and cold—Coming, Cynthia!" She rushed down the steps and across the walk.

"Come on, honey," Francis said, putting an arm around Roxie's shoulders. "Are you shivering, Rox?"

"I think you need to wind her up, Mr. Cable," Bess called. "I declare, she's been standing there like a statue all this time! Are you all right, Roxie?"

"Honey, you're cold," Francis said. "Now, let's get in the car and not keep the nice folks waiting."

I'm finally getting to leave the house alone. Meet me . . . Meet me . . .

"Daddy, there's something I have to do—" Roxie said.

"Aw, but there isn't anything that can't wait until after church now, is there?" Francis asked.

Roxie felt his fingers, tight on her arm. She looked from his face to the crowded car at the end of the driveway.

Meet me . . . You'll just be a little late, is all . . . Meet me . . .

Roxie swallowed hard and found her voice.

"Nothing that can't wait, Daddy . . ." she said. There was a flash of a second in which she saw herself tearing down the walk, running as fast as she could, running to make up the time she'd lost. But she followed her father toward the open car door.